The Foundling

A Tale of our Own Times
by Captain Tree[1]

Charlotte Brontë

ET REMOTISSIMA PROPE

Hesperus Classics

Hesperus Classics
Published by Hesperus Press Limited
4 Rickett Street, London sw6 1ru
www.hesperuspress.com

First published by Hesperus Press Limited, 2004

Designed and typeset by Fraser Muggeridge
Printed in Italy by Graphic Studio Srl

isbn: 1-84391-098-5

CONTENTS

PREFACE

I here present the reading public of Verdopolis[2] not with a fictitious narrative but with plain relation of facts. The events commemorated in the following pages are incidents which, within this last year, have occurred within our own city. I am sensible that my tale is totally devoid of interest, but it may not perhaps be considered egotistical in me to say that it contains none of those vile and loathsome falsehoods, those malignant and disgusting insinuations with which some late writers have thought proper to adorn their contaminating pages. I have, however, scotched one small reptile,[3] as it were, en passant. My little volume is now in the hands of the public and I hope it will find favour in their eyes.

CAPTAIN TREE

About twenty years since, there stood in a retired corner of that part of merry England called Derbyshire, a little thatched cottage whose whitewashed and honeysuckled porch and gay, neatly decorated garden proclaimed to the occasional passenger that its inhabitants were not so hardly pressed by penury as to be wholly unmindful of those little tasteful luxuries which contribute so materially to the happiness of every rightly formed mind. The landscape which encircled this nest of apparent contentment was bounded to the north by a long rugged range of hills, from the midst of which the Peak rose like a dim azure cone. To the west and south extended a flat rich plain watered by the fertilising Derwent, and to the east the narrowed view was bounded by a stately grove of oaks which concealed Oakwood Hall, the venerable family mansion of a neighbouring gentleman.

It was on a stormy evening in the latter end of September that John Cartwright and his wife Margaret, were seated under the roof of this little hut where they had resided for more than forty years, as happy as any two wedded human beings can expect to be in this world of cares and uncertainty. The fire burnt bright and cheerily; the hearth, the floor and the glittering dresser were evidently under the management of an ultra-clean housewife. John had been perusing for the last two hours a respectable-looking volume of divinity, whose elongated black type and jaundiced complexion said as plainly as they could speak that their owner was no flimsy ephemeral production of modern days, but one on whom Antiquity had set his seal; a book which had stood the wear and tear of many generations. At length he closed it with an emphatic yawn and turning to his wife, asked if supper would soon be ready. Margaret, who had already laid aside her knitting materials, answered in the affirmative, and immediately began to busy herself in the preliminary arrangements. In a few minutes, bread, cheese and a tankard of home-brewed were on the table. John drew forward his chair and lifting up his hands, was just about to implore a blessing, when a sudden cry without arrested the prayer which stood on his lips. He started. Margaret turned pale.

'What is that noise?' said she in an affrighted tone.

'I can't tell,' replied John, 'but hearken, perhaps we shall hear it again.'

They listened attentively. Nothing was heard but the wind and rain which fitfully moaned and pattered among the falling leaves.

They were about to recommence their supper when a piteous wailing sound, like the cry of a distressed child, rang on the blast. John rose and opened the door. He looked out into the night, but all again had subsided to utter silence.

'This is summat strange,' said he. 'Hollo there, who are you, and what do you want?'

'Mam, mam, mam,' said a voice close at hand.

John hastily retreated into the house, exclaiming as he shut the door, 'Goodness guard us, that's not a language spoken by flesh and blood. There's either a ghost or a fairish[4] in the garden.'

Margaret, however, was of a different opinion. She took the candle and went out, while her husband, afraid of appearing less courageous than his wife, soon followed her. After a short search, they descried a covered basket under some rose-bushes. While they were gazing at it in astonishment, the cover lifted up and a tiny hand was protruded from underneath.

'As sure as I'm a living woman,' said Margaret, 'there's a ba'rn[5] i' that basket,' and seizing it as she spoke, she hastily re-entered the house.

When the door was carefully closed and bolted, she and her husband proceeded to examine their prize, which turned out to be neither more nor less than a pretty, delicate-looking little child of about twelve months old. The sweet, confiding smile, which beamed in its large blue eyes and dimpled its rosy cheeks, completely won the hearts of the worthy couple. Margaret kissed and embraced it with maternal fondness, and John promised that while they lived it should never more want a roof to shelter its head. That night they retired to rest, the happiest pair in England. The drop of bitter which had hitherto mingled with their cup of sweets was the want of a child to share their affection while living, and inherit their small property after death should have removed them to a better world. This cause of complaint seemed now to be almost miraculously taken away, and their felicity was for the time unmingled.

On the afternoon of the next day, Margaret was sitting at the cottage door with the child on her knee when Mr Hasleden, the proprietor of Oakwood Hall, passed by. This gentleman was a bachelor between fifty and sixty years of age and possessed of an estate whose annual income was about three thousand pounds. He stopped on perceiving the child and exclaimed in a tone of astonishment, 'Whose bonny ba'rn is that, Margaret?'

'It's mine, sir,' said she, rising and curtseying.

'Yours! Why I never knew you had one.'

'No, not until last night, when John and I found this sweet lamb in the garden under that rose tree by the gate.'

'Then you don't know whose it is?'

'No indeed, but as it seemed fatherless and motherless, we thought we'd take it for our own like.'

'Is it a boy or a girl?'

'A boy, sir. I found a paper pinned to its frock this morning with the name Edward Sydney written on it.'

Mr Hasleden, after reflecting a moment, said, 'Dame Cartwright, I'll take the charge of that child's maintenance on myself. You may nurse it if you will and be its foster mother, in which capacity you shall have ten guineas a year as recompense for your trouble.' So saying he departed, without waiting for her answer.

She felt a strong disinclination to resign her right to the little foundling, and half determined to resist Mr Hasleden's claim. However, when her husband returned from his work in the evening she informed him of what had passed, and asked his advice. He gave it without hesitation in the following words. 'I'll tell you what, wife, it's my opinion that we should be behaving unjustly to the ba'rn if we refused such a grand offer, for I believe it's of quality birth, look at yon silk mantle that it was lapped in when we fun it last night. The thingumy 'at fastens it is some mak of a precious stone judging by its glitter, and no poor body could own such a one. I think we ought to give Mr Hasleden the cloak, for it might be of use in proving his birth some time.'

Margaret, like a dutiful wife, succumbed to her husband's arguments, and that very night she walked up to Oakwood Hall for the purpose of delivering the cloak into Mr Hasleden's own hands. He commended her honesty and foresight highly and taking the mantle carefully, locked it up in his strongbox.

Years passed on and the secret remained unravelled. Edward Sydney sprung up into a handsome boy, still, however, retaining that delicacy of appearance which had distinguished his infancy. But he now began to evince dispositions which showed that his was no common origin. There was in his character a decision which, according as it was properly or injudiciously managed, might form the foundation of a noble character or degenerate into one of dogged commonplace obstinacy. Generally mild and affable to those about him, he could sometimes, when opposed, assume a glance and tone of proud unbending haughtiness that spoke of noble blood. Mr Hasleden, who still continued his kind and generous protector, attentively observed these peculiarities and pursued that system of treatment which was best calculated to cherish his excellencies and repress his defects. He was never irritated by unnecessary opposition or spoilt by foolish indulgence. At the age of ten years he was sent to Eton College. Here his naturally fine abilities rapidly unfolded themselves. Eagerly and unremittingly he laboured in the attainment of every branch of learning which could contribute to the formation of an accomplished scholar. His efforts were rewarded with distinguished success, and before he left Eton he attained the rank of captain and received his tribute of salt at the montem.[6] Cambridge and Oxford next opened their portals for his still on-journeying spirit. He chose the latter temple of learning and remained within its gates until he had grasped the highest academic honours. Scarcely was the last laurel wreath twined round his brow when he received a sudden summons to repair immediately to Derbyshire on account of his father's (for in this relationship he had always been taught to suppose Mr Hasleden stood with regard to him) illness. He arrived just in time to close his eyes and receive his dying blessing.

For many weeks deep sorrow rendered him totally

regardless of all external concerns. In Mr Hasleden he had lost his earthly all. Not the slightest interest did he now feel in any human being, for John and Margaret Cartwright, whom he had loved with the truest affection, had many years since been gathered to their fathers. But the spirit of youth is elastic. Adverse fortune may temporarily bow it to the very earth, yet it soon springs back to its former position and remains as upright as if the blighting finger of Grief had never touched it. When the first comfortless cloud of mourning had passed away, Edward began to seek employment in the examination of his father's papers. The first he opened was his will. All the property was bequeathed to him as his only son. He glanced listlessly over it and having ascertained the tenor of its contents threw it back into the escritoire and took up a small parcel sealed and directed to himself. It contained a crimson silk mantle fastened with a splendid jewelled clasp, and a paper which unfolded his real name and related the circumstance of his discovery. When the influence of astonishment had in some degree subsided, he could not withhold a few bitter tears on learning that the man whom he had so long loved and looked up to as a father was in reality no more than an unconnected though most generous friend. The next feeling which occurred was curiosity respecting his true origin, which the cloak and costly diamond clasp induced him to imagine was rather exalted. And now that bright hope of future fame which had cheered him on during his past career came soothingly over his spirit. He wandered pensive, but not unhappy, through the almost desolate apartments of Oakwood Hall, cherishing dreams of renown, and pondering the most direct means of accomplishing their realisation.

The peaceful tranquil character of the times in which he lived was unfavourable to rising talent. England was still almost stagnant; his ardent spirit longed to be tossing on the stormy ocean of political or martial contention. He felt no inclination to sit down and earn the quiet bloodless laurels due to literary pre-eminence. Active exercise of his corporeal, as well as intellectual, powers seemed necessary for the complete gratification of his desires. With these feelings, he mentally glanced over the world in search of some land whose internal condition might quickly call to life his slumbering faculties. None appeared so likely to afford the necessary stimulus as the distant and, to an Englishman, almost Utopian, colony lately founded in Africa, which was rising like a New Albion under a brighter sky and sunnier climate, peopled – so at least report said – by a race of men widely different from all others on the habitable globe. The species of mystery which hung over its concerns gave it an additional charm in Sydney's eyes. His resolution was immediately taken. He determined to quit England for ever and pursue glory in regions more likely to be blessed by her presence.

'Yes,' he exclaimed with raising enthusiasm. 'If I come from a patrician stock, I will never disgrace my ancestry. If of a plebeian one, my deeds shall ennoble it.'

As he spoke these words he was standing alone in the dusky twilight by a lofty arched window which looked on the dark girdling woods that surrounded his mansion. He started as a faint breeze brought these words to his ear, spoken in a far-off aerial tone like an articulate whisper of wind: 'Son of the illustrious, do as thou hast said.' The voice and breeze died away together. Edward gazed out on the night, but his eyes met nothing except tall gnarled branches swaying slowly to and fro. He retired to rest, and his dreams that night were full of the loftiest aspirings with which ambition ever fired a human breast.

2

'And that is Verdopolis! That splendid city rising with such graceful haughtiness from the green realm of Neptune. Queen of Nations, accept the homage of one who seeks but to be among the number of thy slaves!'

Such was Edward Sydney's brief but enthusiastic address to our beloved city, as he caught the first glimpse of her proud enduring towers. Scarcely a week had elapsed since he resolved to leave England before he put his resolution into practice, and now, after a month's tossing on the sea, his vessel cast anchor in the Glass Town Bay[7].

It was a lovely day in the beginning of summer when his foot touched Africa's coast, and his eye rested on the Tower of All Nations[8], whose vast outline stood in mighty relief against a deep unclouded sky. For an instant he paused on the quay, and glanced around. Far before him stretched the sea, into which two huge arms branched out from the land and, embracing a portion of its waters, formed the harbour where lay upwards of a thousand vessels of war and merchandise, resting in safe anchorage on its long, rolling waves. The greater part of these ships displayed the lion flag of England, but banners of almost every empire under heaven streamed promiscuously from their mastheads. The busy hum of commerce came softened by distance to land, where it was met by louder and more overwhelming sounds proceeding from those numerous groups which now crowded the quay. Far above him the city walls and ramparts rose to a tremendous height, frowning terribly on the foam-white waves which rushed roaring to their feet. A mingled noise of bypassing multitudes, rolling chariots and tramping horses soared dull and deep over the black battlements. Bells were at this instant announcing the hour of noon, and high above the rest the great cathedral bell sent forth its solemn toll, sonorous as a trumpet's voice heard among lutes and harps.

Verdopolis lay at the mouth of a wide valley which was embosomed in long low hills, rich in hanging groves and gardens, vineyards, cornfields, meadows, etc., etc. The background was closed by lofty peaked mountains whose azure tint almost melted into the serene horizon, and all was faintly seen through a mellowing veil of mist which enhanced instead of depreciating the charms of this earthly paradise.

Sydney gazed on the gorgeous picture until his heart swelled. Then, turning away, he bounded along the quay with the light elastic tread of youthful hope and, after passing the guarded gates, found himself in one of the principal streets of Verdopolis. It was nearly a quarter of a mile broad and apparently of interminable length. One side was occupied entirely by splendid shops, the line of which stretched onward quite unbroken by the interruption of a single private house. On the other side stood an immense range of buildings which, from the beautiful uniformity of their architecture, appeared to be constituent parts of one great edifice. A portico of lofty dimensions stood in the midst, surmounting a great flight of steps which led up to the principal entrance. Here groups of well-dressed figures were seen lounging about, finding in its shade a pleasant shelter from the meridian sun. Servants likewise were visible, passing from one group to another, and handing refreshments on silver trays. From the summit of this colossal building rose a vast dome, supporting a noble sculptured marble lion of proportionate size, which seemed in the act of rising from a couchant posture, and held in one of its gigantic paws a great crimson banner whose mighty folds, waving heavily in the gentle sea-breeze, displayed as they occasionally fell down to perfect stillness on the (at intervals) windless air the words 'Bravey's Hotel'[9], inscribed in bright characters of flaming gold.

The population of this street was various, consisting chiefly of tall, banditti-like men whose muscular frames and weather-beaten brows spoke of active and constant exercise in the open air. Smart jaunty personages, attired in military costume, passed among these with the dashing step and bearing peculiar to their profession. Now and then a superior-looking cavalry officer galloped by on horseback. A tolerable sprinkling of bucks and bloods were also observable strutting up and down. But the portion of this motley assembly which most attracted Sydney's attention was some odd little specimens of humanity averaging about four feet in height, whereof those who appeared to be of the male gender were dressed in black three-cornered hats, blue coats, red waistcoats ornamented with large white buttons, black breeches, white stockings and one great round wooden shoe on which they shuffled about with marvellous rapidity. The women wore blue gowns, red jackets, white aprons and little white caps without border or any other decoration other than a narrow red ribbon. Their shoes were similar in construction to the men's. These strange beings were seated at low stalls which they had raised on the pavement, and which were filled with stockings and mittens of lambswool, spun linen towels and napkins, eggs, salt butter and fish, water melons, dried herbs, etc., etc. They called out to every passenger, 'Daw mun boy for t' saak and kluke,' and occasionally some of the men, when unemployed, amused themselves by singing the following exquisite stanzas:

Eamala is a gurt bellaring bull,
Shoo swilled and swilled till shoo drank her full,
    Then shoo rolled abaât
    Wi' a screeaâm and shaât
And aât of her pocket a knoife did pull.

And wi' that knoife shoo'd a cutt her throit
If I hadn't gean her a strait waist-coit.
    Then shoo flang and jumped
    And girned and grump'd
But I didn't caâre for her a doit.

A sooin shoo doffed her mantle of red
    And shoo went and shoo ligged her da'ân at h' bed,
    And therre shoo slept
Till a' th' haâse wor swept
And all the gooid liquar wor gooan fro her head.[10]

As Sydney was listening to a little burly fellow chanting this delectable strain, he heard the sound of a drum and fife behind him, and on turning round saw the following unique procession advancing up the street. First came an immensely tall and powerful man whose gaunt overgrown form was clad in a suit of faded crimson velvet, adorned with tarnished embroidery; he wore a small sword at his side, and a dirty white feather in his hat. Behind him came a wagon covered with black cloth and drawn by two apologies for horses; on each side of this gloomy vehicle two young men bounded forward in a dancing step. The countenance of one of them would have been handsome had it not been for the legible and ghastly lines which famine had imprinted on every feature. The other's pale, thin face and sharp eyes had an expression

13

of low craftiness which was a little repulsive to Sydney's feelings. Both the youths were scantily clothed in torn remnants of finery. Their feet and legs were, however, quite destitute of covering, and their heads were only protected from the scorching sun by a ragged red handkerchief tied round them. These were followed by two musicians, one bearing a drum and the other a fife, and the procession closed by a string of some twenty or thirty naked, lean, miserable-looking children, some of whom were covered with blood and long weals, apparently the effect of recent stripes. When they reached the hotel vestibule, their leader called a halt. The wagon immediately stopped; the black curtains flew open, and the horrid apparition of a living skeleton sprang from under them. It bore in its bony fingers a brazier full of burning coals which it placed on the ground.

The leader now exclaimed to the crowd which was fast assembling, 'Gentleman, he's now going to show you a feat which has never been performed and never will be again.' So saying he made a sign. Two of the enfants instantly leapt into the fiery brazier. The skeleton raised it to his head without any apparent effort, and commenced dancing to a tune which the musicians at this moment struck up. The enfants lay for an instant motionless, then, starting up, they continued to cut capers of half a yard high and fling themselves into all imaginable attitudes, until their extremities were entirely consumed. Pigtail,[11] for he (as my readers will have already guessed) was the master of this strange band, then commanded skeleton to remove the brazier and to bring him two hooks from the wagon. These orders were executed as soon as delivered. Pigtail took the hooks, and summoning two more enfants thrust them each through the middle. In this state he held them dangling at arm's length. They immediately commenced a series of doleful shrieks, which they modulated in such a manner as to resemble a tune, to which Young Napoleon and Eugene danced a pas de deux.

Sydney, who had watched the first exhibition with feelings of such deep horror as had rendered him unable to stir, now rushed forward from the crowd. 'Wretch,' cried he, advancing to Pigtail, 'How dare you thus brutally murder innocent children in the open street, and how, gentlemen' (addressing the crowd), 'how can you behold such infernal barbarity unmoved?'

A general horse-laugh was the answer to his query. Pigtail grinned a ghastly smile and seizing him around the waist, prepared to thrust him into his black wagon. Sydney resisted, but in vain. He called on the spectators to defend him, and was only replied to by such exclamations as these: 'Huzza, Pigtail – in with him – the English bug, how couldn't we find him out before?' 'We'll have no vermin teaching and preaching in our streets.' 'Sweep the pest from the face of the earth.' 'I say, Ned, fetch me a pair of tongs and I'll help to put him to bed.'

Sydney still continued to struggle, though faintly, when the sound of horses' hoofs was heard approaching, and two gentlemen galloped swiftly up and, on hearing Sydney's cries for assistance, they both stopped. One of them asked what was the matter. 'Nothing,' answered a rare lad, touching his hat to the enquirer, 'but an Englishman singing over his deserts.'

'Hold your tongue you scoundrel,' answered the gentleman, 'I'll knock your teeth down your throat if I hear any more impudence.'

So saying he pushed up to the wagon and, drawing a loaded pistol from his belt, commanded Pigtail to deliver up his prey on pain of instant death. Pigtail, who dreads firearms, sulkily complied, and then, collecting his train, moved off. Sydney, thus preserved from captivity or perhaps death, proceeded to thank his deliverer in the warmest terms which gratitude could suggest, but he was greatly discouraged on perceiving that they were received with a mixture of cold politeness and contempt.

'I should like to know, sir,' said the gentleman in reply, 'what brought you into such a pickle?'

'I merely attempted to remonstrate with that horrible monster respecting his treatment of some innocent children whom he was cruelly murdering.'

'A stuck pig, meddling ninny,' observed the other gentleman, who now spoke for the first time. 'Come on, Douro,[12] you surely won't spend any more time in talking to such a whey-faced whiner.'

'Hold your tongue, Jem, or else bite it off,' returned Douro. 'I want to know where this unhappy heap of mortality is going. I say, sir, in what direction will you turn your charming phiz now? You look very much in doubt as to the matter I fancy.'

'Really, sir,' replied Sydney, who felt extremely annoyed at this supercilious deportment, 'I do not know what right you have to ask me such a question.'

'The right of might,' said Douro as he leapt lightly from his horse and threw the reins to his companion. 'Come, my lad, you and I must not part in this way. I see by that flash in your eye that you're worth preserving.'

'Sir, I will not be detained,' exclaimed Sydney as the Marquis seized his arm.

'But you shall, sir, and that as long as I please. Here, Tom!' addressing a tall lusty fellow who stood grinning by. 'Take this luggage and bear it off to Waterloo Palace; ask them to show you the way to my library; there leave it, and tell the servants to supply him well with food until I come home.' So saying he remounted his horse, politely bowed and smiled to Sydney, and, striking his spurs into the courser's sides, was out of sight in a moment.

The rare lad took Sydney in his arms and carried him off with the same ease as he would have done a child. A burst of laughter from all the spectators who were not yet dispersed saluted the indignant youth's ears as he was borne triumphantly away. Burning with rage and shame, he strove to struggle, but in vain; his limbs were so tightly confined by Tom's muscular arms that he could not stir a finger. After passing over six miles of ground, they reached a splendid palace which was situated at the summit of a lofty hill which on one side fell sheer down to the sea in a perpendicular precipice two hundred and fifty feet high. Huge oaks and cedars grew on its brink, some of them so lofty that their topmost boughs swept the palace dome. Lawns and gardens with groves of palm and myrtle covered the rest of the hill, while acacias, weeping willows and other drooping trees grew gracefully on the banks of an artificial river or canal which circled its base. Tom presently crossed this by means of a small bridge. Rapidly mounting the eminence, in a few minutes he reached a wall which hid from view the numerous offices and outbuildings, and here he halted and called out, 'Hollo Bill, let me pass.'

'What do you want then?' replied the gruff voice of a sentinel who now appeared at a great iron gate.

'To do the Marquis's pleasure,' said Tom.

The gates instantly unfolded and Tom passed without further examination. After traversing two wide courts paved with coarse grey marble he arrived at a massive portal of the same material. Tom rung a bell, and, opening as if by magic, he passed on through an intervening hall and then entered the kitchen. This was an immense apartment illuminated and warmed by a huge rousing fire from whose appropriate cauldrons, spits and ovens issued a most savoury perfume of roast, baked and boiled. Ten or twelve kitchen maids and scullions were flitting about, engaged in the preparations for dinner as it was now past seven o'clock p.m. At the head of a great oak table sat a starched, stately old lady, attired in rustling black silk. She appeared to be the presiding deity of the place and gave forth her orders with a dignified majesty and manner that might have done honour to a higher situation. Tom advanced with his burden to this important-looking personage, and in a very respectful tone requested to be shown the way to the Marquis of Douro's library.

'What kind of goods have you got there?' said her ladyship, drawing herself up.

'Nothing at all, Mrs, but an English nincompoop that the Marquis wishes to be kept locked up in his library and well crammed with victuals until he comes home.'

'Well, set him down. Two of the servant wenches can carry such a silly fellow as that upstairs.' Tom, however, demurred to this arrangement, and Mrs Cook, being in a complaisant humour, directed a chambermaid to show him the way.

After ascending staircases and crossing many halls, corridors, galleries and antechambers, they reached the library at last. Here Tom deposited his charge and after a sound kick and curse, shut the door and locked it after him. Sydney thus left to himself began to find food for the most bitter reflection. He was alone in a strange country whose inhabitants seemed more wild and lawless than the rudest barbarians, in the hands of one who, to all appearance, was possessed of nearly despotic power and who, judging by his present exertion of it, seemed disposed to stretch it to the uppermost. His dreams of glory were likewise fast fading.

How could he possibly attain eminence among a people who appeared to regard him and all his fellow-countrymen with contempt and abhorrence. This question he only answered with a deep sigh, and vowed, if he ever should escape from his present unjust imprisonment, to return home and strive to be content with whatever lot might there befall him. But what rankled deepest in Sydney's proud heart were the insults to which he had been so publicly exposed. Involuntarily he ground his teeth as he thought of it and swore to be revenged. He then rose and proceeded to examine his prison to see if there was any means of escape. None, however, offered. The door was locked; the windows were secured by gold lattices and, even if he could have removed these, the height from thence to the ground was so tremendous that nothing could have prevented his destruction if he had attempted to leap it. Sorrowfully he turned away and throwing himself on a sofa, glanced for the first time at the splendid decorations which surrounded him.

The books which lined this magnificent apartment were concealed by a drapery of sea-green silk tastefully arranged on the walls and gathered together at the roof in the form of a dome, the silken flutings of which were confined by a large crystal ornament shaped like a sun. From this depended a small but exquisitely elegant lustre, the branches of which were polished silver and the drops clear sparkling crystal. At each of the four corners stood a white marble bust being representations of the greatest British poet, philosopher, statesman and historian, viz: Milton, Newton, Pitt and Hume. In a recess on one side of the mantelpiece stood a pair of very handsome globes, and in a corresponding recess on the other there was a large telescope with its stand on a round table of dark polished rosewood. In the middle of the room lay writing materials and a confused heap of pamphlets, tracts, newspapers and half-bound volumes which, when Sydney had examined, he found to be chiefly of a political nature. One work lay open, with a silver pencil case and a cambric handkerchief beside it. Sydney glanced at a paragraph which was marked and was to this effect. 'The commodity in which our party is deficient is rising young men. A firm phalanx of fiery, talented youths would do more to secure the victory than all the grave deliberative sages on earth. These should be obtained at any risk or price, and all who do not wish to see the aristocracy of Verdopolis trodden underfoot by an upstart demagogue and his dirty crew should unceasingly exert themselves to enlist, or even impress if necessary, recruits of this description.' Sydney closed the work with a smile. 'I see now,' said he, 'why I have been so unceremoniously treated, but this is a strange country where men may be thus seized and detained without their own consent, to serve the purposes of some political party.'

With a lightened heart he returned to the window and, gazing through the lattices, watched the setting sun which, as it slowly disappeared, suffused sea and land with a glorious crimson blush. As the last golden ray was vanishing, a small bell sounded in the apartment. Sydney turned round. His astonishment was great on perceiving that every book and pamphlet had been removed from the table, on which was now arranged a small but choice repast, served up in the most beautiful porcelain covers, with silver salts, spoons and forks. No one, however, was visible. The door was still closed. Not the slightest noise had been audible while the cloth was being laid. He was almost tempted to think himself in the hands of magicians or genii who, he had heard, yet retained their influence over the inhabitants of Africa. But this idea did not prevent him from doing ample justice to the good cheer thus opportunely provided. He had eaten nothing since morning and therefore had a right to be hungry. When he had finished he took a book and sat down on the sofa. He had scarcely read two pages when the bell sounded again. He hastily looked. The dinner things had disappeared and two decanters, a wine glass, a silver basket of grapes, and a dish of cakes stood in their place. More surprised than before, he returned to the table, took a single glass of wine and a few grapes, then resuming his former seat he determined to watch until the dessert should vanish. Night, however, came on and it still remained. Drowsiness now attacked him. He struggled against it for a while but at length, resigning himself to its pleasing influence, he sunk to sleep, and in a few minutes a dream conveyed him back to Oakwood Hall.

3

On awaking the following morning, Sydney found himself stretched on a soft couch over which hung a canopy of crimson velvet. He drew the curtains. The first object that met his eyes was his own portmanteau, which he had left on board the ship when he quitted it yesterday at noon. 'Surely,' he exclaimed, springing from the bed, 'the stories of enchantment are not all false or how could this box be brought here without my knowledge, how could I be moved from one room to another without awaking?' He comforted himself, however, with the reflection that as yet no harm had been done, nor did any appear to be intended.

After changing his dress and adjusting his hair by the help of a splendid mirror, he looked round to see if there was any mode of exit from the chamber; a door stood ajar. He passed through it, and after crossing a short gallery re-entered the library where he had fallen asleep the preceding night. Here all was in exact order. A cheerful fire burnt in the grate, and an elegant breakfast was laid out on the round table. He ate sparingly, and then took up a newspaper which lay damp and folded beside his coffee cup. His attention was immediately arrested by the following paragraph: 'We understand that a prime young English cock was picked up yesterday by the Marquis of Douro in Hotel Street. If he answers well, and the Marquis is seldom mistaken in his guesses, let Lord Ellrington[13] look to it!' Sydney dropped the paper with astonishment, which was increased on perceiving that the breakfast table was entirely cleared. He rose, paced the room for a few moments in evident agitation but at length, composing himself, he took up a book and resumed his seat. The volume he had chosen was a novel by Captain Arbor.[14]

The plot of this work happened to be one of uncommon depth and interest, and he soon became absorbed in its perusal. The hours which might otherwise have been tedious now flew rapidly by, and before he was aware the dinner bell again sounded. All had been prepared as usual by some invisible power.

When he had completed his meal, he remained at the table, determined to see how the process of removal was conducted. After a short pause of expectation he observed a slight agitation of the silk tapestry. It was silently lifted, and a living creature (for I cannot call it a man) advanced from underneath. This strange being stood about three feet high. His huge head was covered with a shock of coal black hair, his horrible features received additional hideousness from a pair of small bead-like eyes in which gleamed an expression of fiendish malignity. The rest of its deformed person was concealed by a dark mantle reaching to its large splay feet. When Sydney had a little recovered from the slight tremor into which this apparition had thrown him, he respectfully addressed it, but the creature returned no answer either by word, look or sign, as it proceeded to remove the dinner things, sweeping them with marvellous celerity and utter noiselessness into a matted tray which it bore on its head. Having completed this business, it glided behind the tapestry and disappeared as it had entered.

Several weary days passed, and Sydney saw nothing but this frightful dwarf, which appeared at stated periods, performed its duties, and departed. He was beginning to be heartily tired of his luxurious prison when one afternoon he received a visit from rather a different person. His attention was attracted by hearing the hangings rustle at an unusual hour, and on glancing hastily and rather angrily towards them, the form of a beautiful young lady met his astonished gaze. She was rather tall. Her hair and eyes were very dark, and her complexion delicately fair. On perceiving Sydney she blushed, curtseyed gracefully, and was about to retire when he started up and, in an earnest manner, implored her to stay. She complied with evident reluctance.

'Madam,' said he, 'you will no doubt be extremely surprised to find me in this apartment and I assure you it is very much against my own inclination that I remain here.' He then related the circumstances of his capture and subsequent imprisonment and concluded by entreating her to furnish him with the means of escape.

'Ah,' said she with a sweet smile, 'I see you are an Englishman and do not know the country. Believe me when I say that no harm is intended you, but, on the contrary, good.'

'Yet, madam,' replied Sydney, 'is it not unjust to confine an unoffending stranger thus rigorously?'

'No,' said the lady promptly, 'not when some ample recompense is about to be made him which I am sure is your case.'

This answer did not satisfy Sydney and he again requested her to set him at liberty.

'Set you at liberty!' she exclaimed with great vivacity, 'I will do no such thing! What would the Marquis say when he came home and found the nest empty and the bird flown? Truly, my head, in such a case, were he to discover that I had been the deliverer, would not be worth a straw.'

'But fair jailor, for so I must call you, since you refuse to emancipate me, how could he find out that circumstance?'

'Oh, his lordship is more sharp-sighted then Argus. Let no one ever hope to escape his vengeance by perpetrating their acts of disobedience in secret, his vigilance will be sure to find out the offender, though he were hid in the centre of the earth. Besides, sir, leaving these weighty considerations out of the question, my own conscience would never forgive me were I to displease him.' So saying she dropped another graceful curtsey and quitted the room, leaving Sydney in a more desponding mood than ever.

Another week passed in the same monotonous manner. He now almost despaired of regaining his liberty. Confinement and solitude weighed heavily on his spirits, and his health suffered not a little from want of exercise. On the fifteenth morning, as he was pensively entering the library, he started on perceiving the Marquis seated at the breakfast table and engaged in perusing a newspaper. As Sydney came forward, he rose, advanced to meet him with that bewitching smile which he so well knows how to assume, and frankly offering his hand, addressed him thus: 'Well my good fellow, I am at last come to set you free. Nothing I assure you but the most urgent business could have prevented me from visiting you long since, and I did not choose to send orders for your release because, as you are an Englishman, and totally unacquainted with the manners of our citizens, I knew that you would be continually getting into scrapes, some of which might have proved fatal to you before assistance could be procured.'

Sydney, though the wounds his pride had received still continued unhealed, could not resist the cordial politeness of the Marquis's manner. He bowed, and thanked him for the interest which he appeared to take in his welfare, but, at the same time, hinted that no good office would be so agreeable as an immediate restoration to liberty. The Marquis smiled again and replied, 'Your wishes shall be attended to. I have no desire to detain you any longer against your inclination, but before you go permit me to ask a few questions. In the first place, what is your name?'

'Edward Sydney.'

'Are you possessed of an independent fortune?'

'My income amounts to three thousand pounds per annum.'

'Is it derived from landed property or commercial concerns?'

'From landed property.'

'Are your parents living?'

'I do not know.'

'You do not know, how is that?'

In reply to this query Sydney briefly related the circumstances of his discovery and explained the mystery which enveloped his origin. The Marquis, after a short pause, resumed his examination.

'How have you been brought up?'

'I have received a university education.'

'Which I presume from your juvenile appearance is not yet completed?'

'Yes, it is. I attained the rank of senior wrangler[15] and took my degree before I left college.'

'Senior wrangler! Why what age are you?'

'Twenty-two.'

A slight blush suffused the young nobleman's fine features at this reply. He answered quickly, 'Why I have been conversing with you all this time as if you were my junior and now it turns out that I am myself three years younger than you.'

Sydney now smiled in his turn as he said, 'Do not be offended my lord, your superior stature and manliness of bearing are sufficient excuses for the mistake.'

'Well, never mind,' replied his lordship. 'I have taken upon myself the office of patron and I will maintain it were you fifty years my senior. Now pray tell me if you would like to be a member of the Commons House of Parliament which represents this great empire?'

'My lord, are you in earnest?'

'Decidedly so.'

'Then nothing would be more gratifying to every feeling of my heart.'

'You would consider that a lucky event which should elevate you to such a post.'

'The most superlatively so of any that ever happened to me.'

'Then know, Mr Sydney, that the business in which I have been engaged during the last fortnight was ousting an obnoxious member from his seat, and procuring your election instead, but now do you know what is required of you as a return for this piece of service?'

'I believe I do.'

'What?'

'A staunch and unflinching opposition to the vile demagogue Alexander Rogue.[16]'

'You have hit the nail on the head in a clever style. Now I have but one question to ask, are you acquainted with the various ramifications of political intrigue which overrun this troubled country?'

'Yes, intimately. I studied them with deep attention before I left England.'

'My dear fellow, you are just the man I desired to find, and hereafter I shall take to myself great credit for penetration – now let us the change the subject. Did your portmanteau reach you safely?'

'Yes, my lord, and great was the astonishment which its

receipt produced. This and some other circumstances almost made me imagine myself in an enchanted palace.'

'Ah, Finick's noiseless attendance joined to his uncouth aspect terrified you a little I dare say.'

'I own that it surprised me, but how did your lordship contrive to discover my trunk?'

'Why, I went down to the harbour and enquired for the last arrival from England. Having gone on board the vessel which was pointed out to me I asked the captain if he had not a young Englishman's baggage in his possession. He delivered up that portmanteau and, as I supposed that you would be inconvenienced by delay in the transmission of its contents, I had it conveyed hither without loss of time. Come,' continued the Marquis starting up, 'will you take a walk through the city? I will be your cicerone and' (smiling) 'your protector likewise until such time as you can divest yourself of that absurd quixotism which makes you the champion of dirty enfants and the antagonist of French tavern masters.'

Sydney, whose resentment had now entirely vanished, readily complied. His noble friend, after conducting him to some of the most magnificent buildings in Verdopolis, proceeded to Bravey's Hotel. Here he secured handsome apartments for him, and after seeing the young senator comfortably installed in his new residence, bade him farewell until the next day.

4

When the Marquis was gone Sydney sat down and began to meditate on his sudden promotion. He had left England scarcely daring to hope that Fortune would so far favour him as to place such an honour within his reach after years of uninterrupted labour, and she had already conferred it on him without an effort on his part. Surely, thought he, some superhuman power must be watching over me and directing events for my good. I feel that I spring from no common root – my own mind tells me so – and then that unearthly voice which called me 'son of the illustrious'. But if ever chance or the fixed course of Destiny shall restore me to my parents (if indeed they still exist), never shall they blush for their son, were they the highest of earthly potentates. These reflections were interrupted by a sudden rap at the door. 'Come in,' said he.

The door opened and an immensely tall and corpulent gentleman entered. He approached Sydney with an air of condescension saying, 'So, are you the young English laddie that's come to take up his quarters in my inn?'

'I believe, sir, that I am the person to whom you allude,' replied Sydney, who regarded his landlord's rosy face and old-fashioned attire, consisting of a cocked hat and laced military surtout of the ancient cut, with considerable curiosity.

'Hum – I am come to tell you that dinner is on the table and that I am going to favour you with my company.' Sydney stared, but answered with politeness that he should feel greatly obliged by the honour. 'Yes, young man, your tongue says so, but not your face. However, it does not much signify to me whether you like it or not. It's my way to do as I please in my own house, so come along.'

With these words he led the way to the dining room, and his astonished guest followed in silence. During dinner few words were spoken on either side, Bravey being actively engaged in the demolition of a fat roast goose, and Sydney in meditating on that unrestrained state of society which could permit a landlord to intrude thus on the privacy of his guests. When the servants had withdrawn, and wine was placed on the table, the old gentlemen began to show signs of an inclination to give tongue. After sundry hems and haws he broke silence thus, 'So, young gentleman, you say you're from England don't you?'

'I do, sir,' was the brief reply.

'Well, don't give such scornful twists to that little nob of yours. I dare say now that you think it's beneath you to dine with me, eh?'

'I assure you, sir, I have not given the matter thought.'

'Oh haven't you! I doubt that, but let me tell you that any Glass Town nobleman, much more an English schoolboy, may think himself highly honoured by receiving such a mark of condescension from one of the glorious Twelves.'

'And are you that Bravey who reflected such splendour by his valour on those illustrious worthies?'

'Yes truly, I am the very fire-eater you mention, who has now thrown away his sword and become pot-valiant[17].'

'Transformed from a hero to an innkeeper? What a change!'

'Oh, there's nothing so very wonderful in it. More surprising alterations take place every day in this mutable world of ours. Besides you must know that it was always the object of my highest ambition, even when I was a poor private in the ranks, to be one day master of a snug pot-house. I ever rejoiced in the bottle' (taking a powerful pull) 'and now in my old age I have no reason to complain when I find myself owner of such a well-frequented public as this.' Sydney assented by a nod, and he continued, 'Now, tell me, lad, what made you come such a long way over the water to our town?'

'A desire to see the world.'

'Doubtless, and perhaps a desire to rise in it too. Eh? Am I right?'

'I do not deny it, sir. The passion of ambition is natural to man, and he who is entirely devoid of it must be either more or less than human.'

'You speak like an oracle, and the Marquis I see has taken you in hand, so I don't doubt that your efforts after distinction will be crowned with success.'

'Sir, is not this Marquis of Douro the son of His Grace the Duke of Wellington?'

'He is.'

'He cannot be more than eighteen or nineteen years of age, I should think from the appearance?'

'About nineteen, I believe.'

'And how is it that one so young is possessed of so much power as he seems to enjoy?'

'Why that is a question of a beardless boy which indeed you are. Does not superior talent always acquire superior influence?'

'Certainly, but I should suppose that the Marquis's talents had not yet had sufficient time to admit of their full development.'

'Nor have they. Enough, however, is known of them to assure the world that no man ever possessed in a more eminent degree the inestimable gift of genius.'

'With so much intellectual wealth, added to the truly fascinating advantages of solid fortune, lofty rank, manners and birth, I marvel that Nature should have given him a person of such faultless elegance, and features so regularly beautiful. Do not you think him surpassingly handsome?'

'Yes he's well enough for that matter, being stronger and more athletic than most of our young noblemen; he's a capital boxer too. But come, you don't take your glass. Where's the use of sitting and prating without moistening one's throat a bit. Here's to the Marquis. Let it be a bumper and no heeltap[18] I beg.'

Sydney willingly drank this toast and then recommenced his series of questions. 'Is the Duchess, his mother, living?'

'No, she died two years since, and long and deeply did the Duke and her children mourn their loss, for a better queen, wife, mother and woman never lived.'

'Has the Marquis any sisters?'

'No, but he has a small imp of a brother.'

'Any likeness in their dispositions and persons?'

'Not the least. Lord Charles is a little vile, ugly, lying, meddling, messing, despicable dirty ape, who delights in slandering all good and great men and in consorting with all wicked and mean ones.'

'Indeed, 'tis strange there should be so wide a difference between two brothers, but I have as yet asked you nothing respecting the Marquis's temper, is it good or the reverse?'

'Hum! Why, I can't justly say, it's half and half I think. To the objects of his regard he's an angel, but to those of his hatred, a very Lucifer.'

'I guessed as much. Those dark eyes of his look as if they could flash fire upon occasion.'

'You would say so if you'd seen him in such awful fits of passion as I have sometimes, darkening and lowering and looking as like a sea storm as possible.'

'You said, I think, that he had no sisters?'

'I did.'

'Then who is the young lady now residing at Waterloo Palace?'

'Really I can't tell. I give myself very little trouble about young ladies. But she's very likely his wife.'

'His wife! Is he married?'

'Yes.'

A long pause followed this short answer. Bravey attempted once or twice to resume the conversation but it would not do. Sydney appeared to have lost all inclination to talk. His spirits seemed to be flagging, so, after about half an hour's silence, the worthy host rose, and bidding him good night, left the apartment.

Sydney continued to sit for a long time deeply absorbed in thought, but at length, as the city bells tolled the hour of eleven, he rose, muttering between his teeth, 'What an absurd fool I am,' then, seizing his candle, he retired for the night.

On the afternoon of the next day he was walking under the vestibule when the sound of approaching wheels became audible and, before he could look up, a magnificent chariot, drawn by four splendid bay horses, dashed forward at a rapid rate. The Marquis, for it was he who drove, stood up as he drew in the reins and bowed to Sydney. He returned the compliment rather slightly, for his attention was a little distracted by the appearance of a young lady who sat beside him. She was dressed in a long violet silk mantle and hat with a long white veil which concealed her face. As the chariot stopped, however, she removed this screen, and he then recognised the well-remembered features of his fair visitant in captivity. The Marquis now summoned one of the hostlers to take the reins from his hand, but, as he was delivering them up, and preparing to alight, the lady detained him saying,

'Now Arthur, do gratify me for this once, and let me drive Hector and the other horses down to the stables.'

'Let you drive Hector and yourself down to perdition!' replied he, gently removing the hand which she had laid on his arm.

Nothing daunted by this decisive answer, she persisted, 'You shall not go now until you give me the reins. I'm sure I can drive as well or better than you, so a truce with these airs of superiority and do as I tell you.'

'Did you ever see anything so obstinate?' said he, appealing to Sydney with a smile.

Sydney who shuddered at the very idea of so fragile-looking a creature undertaking the management of four fiery, prancing blood horses, whom their master with all his skill and strength could with difficulty keep under control, answered, 'I should indeed fear that the lady's courage exceeded her capabilities, and if she will permit me to express my opinion, I would advise her not to dream of attempting an enterprise so full of danger.'

'Ah,' said she, smiling archly, 'You are an Englishman and do not know the ways of this country, but for you, my lord, I can't think what possesses you that you should oppose my will so obstinately. Give me the reins I say once more.'

'Well, Julia, you are a foolish petted girl and must have your own way I suppose, so there they are, now off to the Shades as fast as you can.' He then flung the symbols of government toward her and leapt from the chariot.

She bowed graciously and kissed her hand to him as she assumed the command, but alas, no sooner was she settled in her seat than the high-mettled steeds, who directly felt the difference between her feeble inefficient hold and the Marquis's powerful grasp, began to prance, snort, toss their heads, and show sundry other symptoms of insubordination. Sydney attempted to spring to her assistance, but the Marquis withheld him saying, 'Let her alone. She'll soon be convinced of her incapacity.' Accordingly, after a few faint attempts to soothe and control Hector and the other horses, she turned pale, and looked wistfully towards the Marquis who called out, 'Well, Julia, drive away. What are you standing there for? That's capital coachmanship, my fair knight of the round hat. I could do nothing like that could I?'

'Oh, Arthur,' replied she, in a faltering voice, 'do help me. You see I've not quite got the right way of managing them.'

This appeal was answered by a loud laugh. But Sydney, who was much alarmed at what appeared to him the extreme peril of her situation, freed himself by a sudden effort and running to the chariot snatched the reins from her powerless hands. The jerk which this action occasioned exasperated the chargers still more. They now backened and reared in a frightful manner. Sydney, wholly regardless of his own danger, strove but to extricate the lady who was near fainting with terror. Meantime Arthur stood on the steps laughing heartily at both the charioteers and exclaiming, 'Huzza, my lord Automedon[19]. Bravo my lady Julia. I wish Fred Lofty[20] could see this glorious sport. Hector, my boy, don't give in – sweat them well!' At this moment Hector, as if he had understood his master's words, redoubled his pranks and capers. Sydney could no longer retain the reins. They were wrested from him, and the four horses burst like lightning away. Lady Julia, uttering a faint shriek, would have fallen from the chariot if Sydney had not supported her. The Marquis, now seeing that affairs assumed an alarming aspect, leapt from the summit of the lofty flight of steps and sprang after his rebellious steeds. In five minutes he had reached them. Two words from his lips soothed or awed them into obedience, and when he had succeeded in tranquillising them, he lifted Lady Julia from the chariot.

As soon as she had a little recovered from the effects of her fright, she warmly thanked Sydney for his exertions in her behalf. He, of course, disclaimed all merit on the occasion, but said that nothing could give him so much pleasure as the opportunity of, at any time, serving her ladyship. While these reciprocal compliments were passing, the Marquis, whose merry mood still continued, interrupted them, saying, 'There is no one to be thanked in this business but myself, so cease your palaver. If it had not been for me, you would both of you at this moment be lying dead in the street. Now Julia, my girl, tell me whether you or Lady Zenobia[21] is the most accomplished whip?' Julia hung down her head and began to play with tassels of her mantle. He continued, 'I see you're convinced, so I'll say no more, only, if I had trusted the ribbons to her, with what a noble air she would have mounted the box, grasped the reins and rattled off. If Hector had dared to show her any of his tricks, my word she'd have cut his hide gallantly, and by the by, if she had seen the exhibition of today both you and Sydney would have been cursed for a pair of arrant cowards.'

'Well, my lord, I acknowledge that I don't drive as well as her ladyship. Now you've had triumph so let the matter rest.'

'I will, since you allow her ladyship's superiority at last.'

'Will you return home now, Arthur?'

'Not yet. Go into the hotel and rest yourself for half an hour whilst I accompany Mr Sydney to see the Rotunda[22].' Lady Julia obeyed this command, and the gentlemen proceeded to the Rotunda.

On entering this apartment, which derives its name from its

circular figure, Mr Sydney was forcibly struck with its vast proportions and beautiful dome. The walls, the pillars, and the pavement were all of marble. Velvet couches and ottomans were placed round for the accommodation of guests. On these various groups were reclining, some sipping sherbet and coffee, other playing billiards or cards, smoking cigars etc., etc. As they passed slowly by, some detached words of the conversation that was going forward were audible, such as the following unconnected sentences, 'Jack, if I was you I'd wear a wig!' 'Sir, it's my opinion that the government cannot be maintained much longer if these instigators to rebellion are not immediately put down with a strong hand.' 'You are not playing fair, I saw you look over my partner's hand.' 'My pipe's out.' 'Who's that lad walking with the Marquis of Douro?' 'This state of things will not do. The people are becoming every day more discontented.' 'Only taste this sherbet, Bud. Isn't it abominable?' 'Oh sir, I've no doubt that we shall weather the storm.' 'That conceited monkey Cornet Scrub has just been asking me if I don't think he's in very good face today.' 'My coffee's little better than lukewarm water.' 'How many are you by honours?' 'Where do you buy hair powder?' 'Two to one on Graham.' 'These are not real Havanas.'

As the two friends walked on, the Marquis received and returned many bows, nods, recognitions, shakes of the hand etc., etc. At length they reached a vacant sofa, and when they were seated he addressed Sydney thus: 'I have brought you here, Ned, principally for the purpose of making you acquainted by sight with some of our chief public characters. Now attend to me while I point them out. Do you see that tall grand-looking old gentleman in uniform with gold-framed spectacles and powdered hair? He is talking in a low deliberate tone to yonder lean piece of parchment who stands with one hand scratching his head, and the other blowing his nose. Do you see them both?'

'I do, my lord. Who are they?'

'The former is Colonel John Bramham Grenville, one of the wealthiest and most influential of our gold-gorged merchants, a man of sound common sense and a clear calculating un-muddled brain. His opinion is held by the legislature to be of great importance in all matters of a commercial nature, and he possesses more influence than most men over the movements of the mercantile world. The person with whom he is conversing is Sergeant Bud, a crafty attorney and able counsellor. But his talents lie all in the way of his profession. Out of the law court he is nothing, an awkward idiot, or worse than nothing, an infernal nuisance. Now turn to your right. In that recess under the chandelier sits a gentleman who is perhaps rather under the middle size, but so gracefully formed that you can scarcely perceive the deficiency. His forehead is open, his eye remarkably bright, and his features regularly handsome. At this moment he is examining you through his eye-glass – have you caught him?'

'Yes, what is his name?'

'Captain Arbor, the greatest literary character of this or any other age. He excels equally as a poet, a novelist, a biographer, a dramatic writer, a historian and a satirist.'

'I have read his works, my lord, and can attest the truth of what you say, but who and what is that strange ape-like animal, fantastically dressed in pink and white silk, who now approaches him, and seems attempting, but in vain, to attract his notice by a series of extravagant antics?'

'That, I am sorry to say, calls itself my brother. Do not look at the creature for I am ashamed of its folly. Turn rather to the low, broad old man now entering the room, and calling in a coarse rough voice for a glass of brandy. His clothes, you may observe, are rather of the shabbiest, and his hands not quite so fine and white as a lady's. Look how he shoves away the young bucks crowded round that ottoman and, after driving them off unceremoniously, establishes himself in their places. He has just ejected a masticated quid of tobacco onto Lord Selby's laced coat and now bids him march and not trouble him with his squeamishness. That is Colonel Luckyman, and his name is a brief biography, for never since the world began was anyone more lucky in the accumulation of money than he has been. A sudden rise from poverty to princely affluence has rendered him rather purse-proud, as you may perceive by the manner in which he stuffs his ungloved hands into his breeches pockets, and seems to find in the music of the tinkling cash a full consolation for the openly expressed contempt of that small knot of aristocrats who are quizzing him through their opera glasses. But notwithstanding this defect, he is a worthy, loyal subject, an uncompromising supporter of existing institutions and an irreconcilable enemy to all rash innovators. But stay, there is my worthy friend Bud conversing with John Gifford the antiquary. Do look attentively at that genuine pair of originals. Bud is stout and round-paunched, a lover of good cheer and solid learning, a literatus and an epicure, a soldier and a linguist. His nose blushes with the reflected crimson of the wine cup, and his brow is wrinkled by deep, frequent, and most abstruse meditation. Gifford, on the contrary, is lean, sallow, withered. Antiquary seems written in most legible characters on his forehead. Bookworm gleams in every dim emanation from his small twinkling eye. Mark how contemptuously he handles that beautiful sherbet vase. I don't doubt that he is comparing it in his own mind with some Methuselah[23] of an old broken washing-bowl he has at home, and unquestionably rotten clay makes gilded china kick the beam.[24]'

'They are really two most singular and unique specimens of the savants genus, but your lordship has not yet noticed those two persons who are walking by themselves near the east window. One of them appears every now and then to turn a most sinister eye toward us.'

'Ah! I did not observe *them* before. They form a remarkable contrast.'

'Yes, one is a tall genteel figure with curled auburn hair and brown eyes; his features are too good, though their expression is excessively unpleasant. But the other seems to have been made by Nature when the old lady was out of humour. How hideous are his large gross features, his huge matted head, green demoniacal optics, deformed broad body, long arms and short bandy legs. Who can they possibly be?'

'Those, my dear fellow, are a loving pair of devils incarnate, to wit, Alexander Rogue, Lord Ellrington, and his familiar, Hector Matthais Mirabeau Montmorency.[25]'

Sydney started to his feet. 'And do I see there,' he exclaimed, 'the wretches who are labouring to make Africa a field of blood and to steep her in the life-sap of her children? Oh, my lord, when shall I have an opportunity of declaring to their faces how I detest their deeds, of openly resisting them foot to foot and hand to hand?'

'Tomorrow night,' said the Marquis in a low tone. 'But sit down, Edward, and speak more guardedly. Your words have drawn general observation upon us.'

Sydney resumed his seat in some confusion as he observed that all eyes were turned towards him. Rogue and Montmorency had paused in their walk and were viewing both him and the Marquis with attention. They exchanged a few significant glances, and shortly after left the room. Different persons now began to gather round Sydney and his patron, and as they found that they were no longer secure from intrusion, they presently disengaged themselves from the curious circle which surrounded them and took their departure likewise. Edward retired to his own apartments and the Marquis, after reminding him that he would be expected to make his maiden speech on the following night, proceeded to join Lady Julia, whom he found impatiently awaiting his return. They mounted the chariot which stood at the hotel door, and in two minutes were out of sight.

5

When they were gone Sydney sat down to deep and serious study, partly by the way of preparation for his approaching important trial, and partly to drive away more harassing thoughts from his mind. The truth was, Lady Julia's beauty and sweetness had made a deeper impression on him than he was willing to acknowledge, even to himself. He strove to subdue the incipient passion forming in his heart by reflecting that its object was already appropriated, for he considered her in the light of his friend's wife, and sincerely hated himself for harbouring an idea injurious to one whom he now regarded with the deepest and truest affection. By strong and repeated efforts he at length in some measure tranquillised these tormenting reflections and to prevent their recurrence, proceeded, as has been before said, to occupy his mind with affairs of a more general and public nature. During the remainder of that and the whole of the next day he continued busily engaged in the arrangement of his trains of thought, courses of argument, etc., and had scarcely finished when the Marquis arrived to escort him to the house. In half an hour Sydney had taken his seat, and been presented by the speaker to his fellow members. The ceremony of introduction being over, he began to glance at the persons and things around him.

The hall in which they sat was large and lofty, built in the noblest and most appropriate style of architecture, and displaying everywhere that pure classic taste which he had before remarked as a distinguishing characteristic of the public edifices of Verdopolis. A magnificent chandelier in the midst, aided by numerous smaller ones suspended at equal distances between the pillars, emitted so clear and bright a splendour that everything was seen nearly with the distinctness of daylight. The members were ranged in opposite rows on each side, and the speaker sat under the canopy placed on an elevated dais. For some time the hum of conversation was loud and general but, on silence being commanded, an immediate and profound stillness directly ensued.

The first who spoke was Captain Flower. He moved the order of the day, which was an enquiry into the state of the country, and afterwards proceeded to deliver a speech which, though rather short, still displayed considerable reasoning powers and a fund of sharp, searching satire which seemed to sting those against whom it was pointed to the quick. Sydney thought it sounded like the production of one who was possessed of first-rate oratorial talents, but who had not chosen fully to exert them on that occasion. As he resumed his seat Rogue started up and stepped hastily forward. For a moment he looked keenly and fiercely round, then, with his mantle theatrically flung back, and his tall figure erected in an attitude of haughty defiance, he commenced his harangue.

The first sentences were not spoken in a lower and gentler tone according to the usual custom among orators, but he broke forth at once in a voice of thunder denouncing and anathemising his opponents, calling on the men of Africa to arise and revenge their wrongs by treading their oppressors to the dust; painting in terrible though false colours the pining poverty and squalid misery which he said gnawed the very entrails of his fellow subjects; conjuring the legislature to adopt instant and efficient measures for relief, and threatening them with tremendous consequences in case of their refusing to comply with his injunctions. His whole oration consisted of vague and empty, yet appalling and able declamation, mingled with a few shallow sophisms and an immense number of

downright foundationless falsehoods. This precious exhibition was received with frequent shouts of approbation
from without, and no less frequent groans of disapprobation
from within.

As Rogue concluded, the Marquis, who had been sitting
with folded arms and kindling eyes, muttering at intervals in a
deep smothered voice such interjections as the following,
'Liar, fiend, idiotic rant, villainous trash, etc.,' stepped up to
Sydney and whispered, 'Now, Ned, is your time. Get up
and give the scoundrel a sound drubbing, make haste, for I
see others rising, and don't tremble so or you'll stick.' Thus
urged, Sydney slowly and reluctantly left his seat, quivering
like an aspen leaf, and so pale that he seemed about to swoon.
Several honourable gents were already on their legs, but
the cry for the new member was so general that they at length
gave way.

'Mr Speaker,' he began in a faint and scarcely audible voice.
'I labour under many disadvantages in my present, perhaps
presumptuous, attempt to address the house, which I venture
to hope will be taken into consideration by those who are to
form my audience. I am young and not a native of the country
– a noviciate in this illustrious assembly.'

It is not my intention to follow him throughout the whole of
that splendid speech to which these words formed a timid
introduction; suffice it to say that his success was complete,
was triumphant. Bursts of applause broke out at the close of
every period, completely drowning the feeble serpent-like
hiss raised by Rogue and his adherents. As he went on, he
gradually lost his fearfulness, assumed a bolder tone, and
stepped courageously forth as the champion of law and liberty
and the implacable enemy of rebellion and licentiousness.
With the utmost skill he exposed Rogue's feeble sophisms,

deprecated and disproved his daring falsehoods, and caused his fierce declamation to recoil with tenfold violence against himself. In bitter agony did the arch-demagogue writhe under the torturing lash. A scowl of threatened vengeance contracted his forehead and filled his eyes with unearthly fire, and as the hall shook with the thunders that hailed the young orator as he pronounced his final sentence, Lord Ellrington's powerful voice was heard high above the exulting tumult denouncing terrible and prompt revenge. Sydney heeded not the threat. This was the happiest, the proudest moment of his life. He returned with a light step and flushed cheek to the Marquis, who received him with a cordial pressure of the hand and a warm animated smile, which more fully expressed his approbation than all the words oral language affords could have done. No other person attempting to speak, the question was put and decided almost unanimously in favour of government, not more than sixteen members voting in the opposition.

The speaker then left the chair, and a large concourse of members immediately assembled round the Marquis, loudly congratulating him on the success of his protégé. He said little in reply, but the satisfaction which shone in his eyes amply supplied the place of speech. Sydney was that night introduced to more than one hundred of the principal gentlemen in Verdopolis.

On his return to the hotel, he directly retired to rest, hoping to allay by solitude and silence the intoxications of flattery and triumph which now heated and confused his brain. It was long, however, before he could compose himself to sleep, and when he at length sunk into a feverish unquiet slumber, the voice of applauding senators thundered so incessantly in his dreaming ear that on awaking again he found himself but very little refreshed by this temporary interval of repose.

About a fortnight after this memorable night he received a card from the Lady of Major-General Lord Selby, inviting him to be present at a grand ball and supper she was about shortly to give. Accordingly, at the appointed day and hour, he repaired to that nobleman's splendid residence situated in Sulorac Street. A long cortège of carriages were drawn up at the entrance, many of which were at this moment setting down their fair and noble contents. On his arrival he was shown by a footman up a flight of marble steps guarded on each side by gilded balustrades. At the top of these stood a lofty portal whose ivory folding doors, now thrown open, displayed a magnificent suite of apartments where silken draperies, Persian carpets, costly tables, velvet-covered couches, pictures, vases, statues, etc., seemed vying with each other in the attempt to diffuse around an air of lordly and luxuriant affluence. Groups of richly arrayed figures were seen by the soft brilliance of shaded lamps, moving with stately tread through the perfumed and fragrant atmosphere, while the murmur of many voices arose, speaking in the low subdued key to which politeness restricts colloquial intercourse.

Sydney was announced. He walked in, bowed to the lady of the house, and took his seat on a retired sofa. Anxiously did he gaze on many a fair and lovely countenance hoping to discover the features of his forbidden inamorata. The search, however, was in vain, and he was giving himself up to listless melancholy in the very temple of pleasure, when the Marquis of Douro's name was announced, and that nobleman entered, accompanied by two ladies, each of whom leant on his arm. Sydney's heart sprang to his mouth as in one of these he recognised Lady Julia. She was dressed in a rich dark satin robe, ornamented with a profusion of jewels. A diamond aigrette glittered in her hair, surmounted by a stately drooping plume of white ostrich feathers. Her companion was equally beautiful, but of smaller stature and slighter form. Her features were even more delicate, and so youthful that she did not appear to be above fifteen years of age. She wore only a green silk frock and pearl necklace, and a myrtle wreath twined among her luxuriant auburn ringlets. Lady Julia came forward with a stately inceding[26] tread that might have well beseemed an empress. The other tripped in as lightly and airily as a sylphid or fay. All the company gathered round them as they entered, and it was some time before Sydney could make his way up to them.

At length the Marquis perceived him, and he directly advanced towards where he stood. After the customary salutations he said, 'I believe, Ned, you have seen one of these two ladies before, but have not been introduced to either, and therefore I will perform that requisite ceremony now. This bouncing big girl is my cousin, Lady Julia Wellesley, and this giddy little one is my wife, the Marchioness of Douro.'

Sydney opened his eyes very wide and bowed low, but did not speak. The truth was an overwhelming burden had just been removed from his heart, and now inexpressible joy deprived him of the power of utterance. There is no saying how long he might have stood in the same attitude gazing at Lady Julia if the music had not struck up. It acted as a sort of stimulus, which presently restored him to speech and motion. Lady Selby now informed the Marquis that he was expected to open the dance with any lady he should choose.

'Your ladyship does me great honour,' he replied, 'but I am not yet provided with a partner.'

'Then make haste and suit yourself,' said she, laughing.

'There are hundreds around who would delight to be at your beck.'

He stood looking for a moment, with something of a triumphant expression in his eyes, at the glittering throng which encompassed him, then, advancing to a tall dark handsome woman who was sitting rather disconsolately in a corner by herself, he said, 'If Lady Zenobia Ellrington will permit me the honour of her hand, I shall feel greatly obliged.'

She blushed, started as if the offer had been unexpected, but complied with a smile of evident pleasure. He led her into the midst of the spacious dancing apartment, and while the musicians commenced a slow solemn tune they went together through the courtly movements of a minuet.

Sydney thought that until then he had never known what good dancing was. The Marquis's heroic stature, his graceful yet proud and stately air, united with the almost imperial dignity of Lady Zenobia's form and manner, produced an effect so perfectly harmonious that nothing in the saltatory art could possibly surpass it. But his pleasure at this beautiful exhibition was much diminished when on accidentally looking round, he saw the sinister countenance of Lord Ellrington, who was stationed a little behind the general line of spectators. An expression of cold scorn and hatred deformed his handsome features; suspicion lurked in his eye and brooded on his contracted forehead as, with a furious scowl, he stood regarding his wife and her partner. When the minuet was over, he turned away and appeared to be considering how to act. His resolution was soon formed. After a moment's reflection he approached the young Marchioness of Douro who sat gaily prattling about Arthur to old Lady Selateran. With an air of devotion he bowed and humbly solicited the favour of her company in a single quadrille. She too started and blushed, but not as Lady Zenobia had done. Her countenance assumed an expression of fear, and she attempted to go away without answering. Rogue, however, detained her rather roughly and repeated his request, but before she could reply her husband was at her side. 'What is the matter, sir?' said he. 'What were you saying to this lady?'

'I do not know,' replied Lord Ellrington, with a peculiar smile, 'whether I am obliged to tell you everything I say to such ladies as I choose to honour with my notice.'

'But,' exclaimed the Marquis with an oath, 'you shall tell me or –'

'Arthur, Arthur, don't be so angry,' said his wife, clinging to him in the utmost terror. 'He was only asking me to dance, and I was so silly as to turn away without replying and that displeased him I suppose.'

'No fair lady, it did not displease me, but I trust you will now grant me a favourable answer?'

'Sir, I hope you will excuse me when I say that I cannot comply with your request.'

'And why not?'

'Because I do not think my husband's enemy a fit companion for myself.'

'Oh, if that is your only objection I do not despair of –' he was going on when the Marquis, placing his wife's arm within his own, contemptuously turned his back and walked away.

Rogue then addressed Lady Ellrington. 'Madam,' said he, 'prepare instantly to quit this place and to proceed homewards.'

'Three hours hence,' said she with a determined air. 'I will do so but not until then.'

'What! Am I to be bearded in this by my own wife? Obey my commands this instant or I shall find some method of compelling you to your duty.'

'Ellrington,' she replied calmly, 'I know your motives for acting thus, but be assured I will never succumb to such unjust, such tyrannical treatment. You are sensible that when my determination is once fixed it seldom alters, therefore give yourself no further trouble, for I will not go home – yet.'

Rogue's eyes glared as if they would have started from their sockets. He did not, however, attempt to use force as he had threatened. On the contrary he left the room in silence, and proceeded to another apartment, where wine and refreshments were provided in abundance. There he sat down and began to solace himself with large draughts of the cordial blood of grapes, and at this employment we shall for the present leave him.

Sydney, who had not yet mingled in the dance, now thought he should like to do so, and accordingly he began to look round for a partner. His eye soon lighted on Lady Julia, but on applying to her he found that she was already engaged by a young gentleman, whose countenance he thought he had seen before, but could not exactly tell where nor under what circumstances. Thus disappointed he went and seated himself beside the Marquis who, with his wife and Lady Ellrington, was sitting apart from the rest of the company in a recess. Lady Ellrington was just saying, 'Well, my lord, I suppose it is as much your fault as it is mine that we do not see each other oftener. Why do you never come to Ellrington House?'

'Why, my lady, surely you would not wish me to frequent the house of a man whom I detest and who detests me?'

'Sir, it is not my husband's residence, it is mine, and there I will see any visitors I please without asking his leave.'

'I will not dispute your ladyship's resolution, which doubtless is perfectly just, but as I have no inclination to involve either you or myself in unnecessary fracas with your worthy husband, you will excuse me when I say that I should prefer meeting you in the house of a third person rather than in your own. Now let us change the subject. What makes you so melancholy and so fond of solitude now? In former times you were the life and soul of every party that was so fortunate as to be honoured by your presence.'

'Arthur, that question sounds rather taunting. How can I be otherwise than melancholy when I am united for life to a tyrant, and what pleasure can I find in society where my best and dearest friends regard me with coldness and suspicion because I am the unwilling wife of a demagogue?'

'Yes, but, Zenobia, I once thought you had a spirit which would rise superior to all terrestrial evils, and now you tremble at the frown of a wretch who is scarcely worthy to be your vassal.'

'Arthur, you do not know Ellrington. His anger when once roused is terrible, unappeasable. I have often striven to stand against it but in vain. He always compels me to abject submission in spite of that spirit which you used to call unconquerable.'

'Yet you withstood him bravely tonight, my lady.'

'I did, but it was your presence gave me courage. I resolved that you at least should not see me cowed and degraded by him. But when we return home I shall pay the penalty for my steadfastness and a severe and heavy one it will be.'

There was a long pause and the Marchioness of Douro at last broke it by saying rather timidly, 'I pity you very much, my lady, but at the same time I feel very glad that I am not married to such a hideous and cruel man.'

'I give you envy in return for your pity,' replied her ladyship in a low stern voice.

The Marquis did not appear to notice this brief but very significant sentence. He turned to his wife and said with a smile, 'Marian, how dare you call Lord Ellrington hideous? He is a very handsome man in my opinion.'

'He is not so in mine, though,' replied she. 'His very look frightened me so far from my propriety that I could not muster sufficient sense to frame an answer to his question.'

'Why, you little carping critic, what particular feature in his face do you find fault with?'

'His eyes, I think, though I can't say with exactness, where all are so ugly.'

'His eyes! They are as fine dark optics as any one could wish to see.'

'That does not signify. They are totally unlike yours, not so large, not so bright, not so smiling, and therefore I hate them.'

'And so do I,' said Zenobia with warmth.

'Do you not think, Ned, that I have a right to be vain,' observed he, turning to Sydney, 'when two such women flatter me thus?'

'Indeed I should imagine so, that is, if any man has. But, my lady, the Marquis's eyes are not always smiling. I saw them very much otherwise just now.'

'Did you? Ah! I remember! Well, but it is very seldom that they look so fierce and angry as they did then.'

'Marian knows only one side of my character. I am not often provoked by her, and therefore she is quite ignorant of the lengths to which I can go when passion prompts. But you, Zenobia, know me better.'

'I do, and I admire you more.'

'That is almost impossible,' said Marian very mildly.

'It is not impossible. How can a baby like you appreciate his character?'

The Marquis now interposed. 'Come, come,' said he, 'let us have no quarrelling on so silly a subject, or else I know which I shall admire least. Had we not better join the rest of the company? There is my worthy friend Captain Arbor talking with Lady Selby. I should like to hear their conversation. What say you, Ned, shall we leave this snug nook?'

Sydney bowed assent. They accordingly rose and walked forward, and as they drew near they could perceive that Captain Arbor's fine features were lit up and glowing with enthusiasm as he said, 'Ah, my lady, I trust that while Verdopolis maintains her place among the nations, the voice of song will never be hushed and the chords of the harp never broken. Long may the roar of waves which sounds without her walls be mingled with the melody of minstrels from within. Long may the winds sigh, music-blent round her indestructible towers, and long may the strains of her inspired children be remembered on the earth beneath, until time shall have faded into eternity.'

'Captain,' said Lady Selby, 'I think there is not a heart here present but will respond "Amen" to your prayer. Now will you let us hear those two songs you mentioned?'

'Certainly I will, since your ladyship wishes it. The first is for a male performer and I will sing it myself. It is entitled:

The Swiss Emigrant's Return [27]

Long I have sighed for my home in the mountain,
Far I have wandered, and sadly I've wept
For the land of the stream and the sweet singing fountain,
The land which the torrent for ages has swept.

Back to the rock with its bosom of snow,
Back from the wild rushing river I come,
Still may its waters in melody flow
With moan and with murmur, with ripple and hum.

List to the voice of the far tempest yelling,
Darkly it broods o'er that white icy hill,
Yet its dread music is deep'ning and swelling,
Sounds the loud wind-blast more hollow and shrill.

Stern is the welcome and haughty and high
Which greets my return to the land of my birth,
Thunder peals speak from the heart of the sky,
Pine forests bow to the storm-smitten earth.

Yet to my spirit more sweet is the sound
Than the music which floats over vine-covered France,
When the soft winds of twilight sigh soothingly round,
When stars in the firmament tremble and glance.

And fairer those snowy peaks flash on my sight
Beneath the black veil of that wild heaven above
Than Italy's sky ever cloudless and bright,
Than the sun which shines over that region of love.

There stands the hut where my first breath I drew,
Perched like the nest of an eaglet on high,
Under that lone roof of childhood I grew,
And now I return 'neath its shelter to die.'

Captain Arbor's fine mellow voice admirably suited the air to
which these words were set. A dead hush reigned through the

room while he sang, and even after he had finished the silence remained for some time unbroken, until Lady Selby said, 'Thank you, Captain, you have done yourself justice. The words, the air, the voice were all in perfect and delightful unison. Now produce your other song. I am impatient to hear it.'

'I have it at hand, my lady, but this is best adapted to a female voice. Will your ladyship do us the favour to sing it?'

'Oh no, Captain, I have long given up both playing and singing. You must offer it to some younger lady.'

'Well, then,' said he, 'if the Marchioness of Douro will accept what your ladyship has declined, I should feel much gratified.'

Marian looked at her lord, who whispered, 'It is a love song, I believe, so turn it over to your cousin.' She then said, 'I thank you, sir, for your preference, but as I really think I should not be able to sing the song in a manner at all worthy of its merit, I hope you will excuse me if I refuse the intended honour.'

'Alas!' exclaimed the Captain, 'I am a rejected suitor and know not where to turn next!'

'Why, there is Lady Julia,' said the Marchioness playfully, 'who looks very much as if she would like to be asked.'

'Will you, madam, accept what two fair ladies have capriciously turned away from?'

'Yes,' she answered, 'I will, in spite of Marian's nonsense.'

Captain Arbor then presented the song to her. She stepped forward and gracefully seated herself at a harp which stood near. After preluding a little, as if to ascertain whether the instrument was in tune, she struck out at once into a soft soothing symphony. Her clear flute-like voice rose above the harp's swelling tones, the listeners bent eagerly forward, not a word was spoken, not a finger stirred, while she sang the following:

Serenade

Gently the moonbeams are kissing the deep,
Soft on its waters the yellow rays light;
Waken my love from the visions of sleep,
Bend from thy casement and gaze on the night.

Now heaven is all clear, not a cloud flecks its blue,
Like a bow of bright sapphires it arches the main,
While the cinnamon-perfumed and balm-breathing dew
Wafts scents of Arabia o'er valley and plain.

The bird of the night hath forgotten her song
But hark how the tall trees are whispering on high,
As a soft zephyr passes their branches among
And wakes as it wanders a tremulous sigh.

Stars o'er our pathway resplendently shine,
Dian is leading the hosts of the sky;
Haste then and meet me, my fair Geraldine,
Come, we will walk where the silver sands lie.

Whence came that whispered voice through the still night?
Faintly it sounded, yet sweet in mine ear.
Do thine eyes bend on me their soft dewy light?
Oh say, my beloved, art thou wandering near?

The leafy boughs rustle in yonder dark grove,
A white garment glances and floats on the breeze,
And lo! like a vision of beauty and love
She glides from the shadow of wide-waving trees.

Loud and long was the murmur of applause that rose as the last note died from her lips. Sydney, however, who had been standing close beside her while she sung, did not join in it. She seemed disappointed at his silence, and turning to him asked if he was not fond of music.

'Yes,' replied he, 'devotedly so at all times, but when an angel sings, how can I find words to express the ecstasy of admiration which fills me?'

She now blushed deeply. The gentleman who had been her partner for the night observed it. An expression of vexation crossed his countenance. He looked fiercely at Sydney and seemed about to address him, when the Marquis of Douro, who stood attentively observing the whole group, prevented him by saying, 'Now Julia, can you tell me to whom you have been addressing this fine seranade? There are a couple of gentlemen at your back each of whom seems inclined to appropriate it to himself, and I'd advise you to decide the matter lest there should be a quarrel.'

'A quarrel,' said she, turning hastily round. 'What is the matter?'

'Nothing, madam,' replied Sydney. 'Nothing in the world. I have not yet spoken to your partner nor do I intend to.' So saying he walked hastily away.

Supper was now announced and all the party adjourned to the room where it was laid out. Nothing of importance occurred during this meal, and shortly after its conclusion the carriages were called and the company, with the exception of a few jolly fellows who remained to finish out the night with Lord Selby over a bottle, dispersed. Sydney walked solitarily and thoughtfully to his hotel. When he reached it he retired to bed and dreamt that night of being in Paradise and listening to angels' harps.

6

I trust my reader will excuse me if I now change the scene to Ellrington Hall. About a week after the fête at Lord Selby's, Lady Zenobia was sitting alone in her boudoir when a servant entered and informed her that Lord Ellrington would be with her in less than an hour.

'Very well,' said she, 'I am prepared to receive him at any time.' The servant bowed and left the room.

She sat for some time with her hand resting on her head, and her eyes fixed on a Greek copy of Aeschylus' tragedies which lay before her. This was the first interview she had with Rogue since their quarrel at the ball, and she now dreaded the consequences of his resentment, which she knew would not be softened by delay but, on the contrary, increased in violence, when he should have an opportunity of giving it vent. At first her countenance betrayed no symptom of emotion, but after a little while large round drops appeared trembling in her dark eyes and falling thence to the learned page on which they rested. Presently she started from the table and, hurriedly pacing the apartment, exclaimed in a low tremulous voice, 'What means this weakness? Why do I thus dread one whom I ought to despise? O, that I should ever have resigned myself into the hands of such a man, in a moment of pique at love neglected, contemned, spurned! In an hour of false, fleeting admiration, of abused and degraded talents, I yielded up my liberty and received the galling yoke of worse than Egyptian bondage. Arthur! Arthur! Why did I ever see you? Why did I ever hear your voice? If love for another did not occupy my whole heart, absorb my whole existence, perhaps I might endure the cruelty of this man with less utter, less unendurable misery. Perhaps I might, by unwearied patience, by constant and tender submission, win some portion of his regard, some slight share in his affection. But now it is impossible! I cannot love him! I cannot even appear to love him, and therefore I must hereafter drag out the remnant of my wretched life in sorrow and woe, in hopeless and ceaseless mourning.'

Here she stopped, threw herself on to a sofa, and for a long time wept aloud and bitterly.

Steps were now heard in the corridor. She rose hastily, but before she could assume any degree of calmness, the door opened, and there entered, not Lord Ellrington, but some six or seven young gentlemen,[28] each with a white handkerchief to his face and crying out in the most lugubrious tones, 'Goodbye, sister Zenobia, farewell, adieu, we're all going to be killed, and we've come to see you for the last time.'

'What do you mean?' said she, much alarmed.

It was some time before she could obtain a rational answer from the afflicted band, but at last one of them, who seemed to be the eldest, stammered out, 'We were all dressing and getting ready to go to Viscount Cavendish's boat party when Sylvius began boasting, and saying how much prettier his salmon-coloured coat and dead-white trousers were than Alsana's apple green and French white ones. So Alsana told him that he had no more taste than the washstand, or else he would never dress himself in such vulgar rags, and that beside that his complexion was so horrid that he ought to dress himself in sackcloth and wear ashes on his head, and then Sylvius began to cry, and he cried so long that Alsana pretended to be sorry for him, and he said he would tell him of a cosmetic which should make him fairer than a wax doll. So he told him to get some galls and green coperas[29], to strew them on a wet towel and rub it over his face. So Sylvius pulled out some halfpence and sent a servant to buy the galls and coperas, and when it was brought he did as Alsana had told him, but – lo and behold! – his face, instead of going whiter, turned jet black. When he saw that, he roared out far louder and rougher than a gentleman ought to do, and I told him so. Then he turned on me in a passion, snatched my best fine-embroidered cambric handkerchief out of my hand and wiped his ugly wet eyes on it. Enraged at such a filthy action, I began to pummel him severely. He returned the compliment and we were in the very midst of a furious battle when your waiting-woman came in and told us that Lord Ellrington was drinking with some friends in the room below ours and hearing the noise we made, had fallen into a passion and commanded that every one of us should be carried out into the yard and there beheaded on a log of wood like so many chickens.'

Lady Zenobia could scarcely refrain from smiling at this piteous relation. Sensible, however, that no time was to be lost in providing for her brothers' safety, she ordered them immediately to make their escape by means of a private door which she pointed out, and to hasten to Waterloo Palace, and there implore the Duke of Wellington to protect them until the storm should have blown over.

They were no sooner gone than Rogue arrived in earnest. He entered the room with a firm step, but Zenobia shuddered to see the savage light of intoxication glancing in his at all times fiery eye. Having seated himself, he drew out a pair of pistols, placed them on the table, pulled his wife rudely towards him, and addressed her thus: 'Well, termagant, I suppose you thought I'd forgotten your insolent behaviour to me about a week ago, but I assure you if that was your opinion you're very much mistaken. Kneel at my feet this instant, and humbly and submissively ask pardon for all past offences, or –'

'Never!' said she, while a smile of scorn curled her lips. 'Never will I so far degrade myself! Do not hope, do not imagine that I will!'

'I neither hope nor imagine anything about the matter, but I'm certain of it, at least, if you refuse, an ounce of cold lead shall find its way to your heart. Do you think I will have you dancing and manoeuvring before my very face with that conceited, impertinent, white-livered puppy?'

'Dare not, at your peril, to speak another insulting word of the Marquis of Douro!'

'Fool!' said Rogue, in a voice of thunder, while flames seemed actually darting from his eyes. 'Fool and mad woman, is this the language calculated to screen either you or him from the terrible effects of my wrath? You may grovel now in the dust! You may kneel and implore my forgiveness until your bold tongue rots and refuses to move! I will not grant it now were every angel and celestial and infernal to command me!'

'Base villain, I scorn your forgiveness! I trample your offers of mercy under foot! And think not to harm the Marquis – he is far above your power. That blood-stained, that crime-blackened hand could not harm one hair of his noble head. Yet know, wretch, that though I honour him thus highly, though I look upon him as more than man, as an angel, a demigod, yet rather than break my faith even with you I would this instant fall a corpse at your feet.'

'Liar!' said Rogue. 'These words shall be your sentence and I will execute quickly, but you shall not die the easy death of having your brains blown out. No! I'll thrust this sharp blade slowly through you, that you may feel and enjoy the torture.'

Here he drew a long glittering sword from its scabbard, twisted his hand in her thick black hair, and was just in the act of striking her as she lay unresisting and motionless, when a strong and sudden grasp arrested his arm from behind. Half-choked with fury he turned round. The hideous visage of Montmorency met his fire-flashing eyes, rendered ten times more frightful by the loathsome grin which wrinkled his misshapen features. Shuddering with passion and disgust, he demanded what had emboldened him thus to intrude on his privacy.

'Nothing, my beloved friend,' replied he, 'but firstly the desire of doing you good, and secondly of doing myself no harm. I was walking in the corridor when I heard your dear, well-known voice raised a little above the customary pitch. Anxious to know what could thus have excited my friend, and desirous to share his gratification if the cause were pleasure, and to alleviate his sufferings if pain, I crept on tiptoe to the door. There, by looking through the keyhole, I beheld as pretty a tragedy as one could wish to set eyes on, but when I saw that matters were approaching a crisis, I remembered that the gallows often follows murder, and were we to lose you just now our cause would not soon recover from the shock. My fine dreams of ambition would be in some measure blighted and, moreover, the unfailing spring, the well of the waters of life eternal, whereat I am wont to quench the thirsting of my soul after righteousness, would at once and for ever be dried up. Prompted by these considerations, I magnanimously denied myself the delight of witnessing your play to the end. I stepped forward like a hero, bearded the lion in his wrath, and effected the deliverance of this fair damsel in distress.'

'Well,' replied Rogue sneeringly, 'since the brother of my heart has interposed, I will permit that woman to escape the punishment due to her crimes this once.'

The truth was that Rogue who, though scarcely a man, is not yet altogether a monster, was somewhat moved at seeing the deadly paleness that overspread his wife's face, and the attitude of passive helplessness in which she lay stretched before him. Besides, it must be urged, in palliation of his violence, that the provocation he had received was such as no man either could or ought to have endured in silence. He, however, disdained to show his emotion. Pushing her aside with his foot he exclaimed, 'Get up, heap of baseness, and be gone instantly from my presence!'

She did not attempt to move. He looked at her more closely and found that the fear of death had so far overcome her as to occasion a fainting fit. With a loud and deep oath he rung the bell, and commanded the servant who answered his summons to 'carry that woman away'.

As the man proceeded to obey his orders, Montmorency stepped up and whispered something in his ear, to whom he bowed and answered, 'I will, sir, directly.' In a few minutes he returned with a huge cask of brandy, the head of which was knocked in, and a couple of tumblers. Having deposited these on the table he again left the room.

Rogue did not appear to consider this strange freedom of Montmorency's as anything at all uncommon. They both drew near the table and, dipping their tumblers in the cask, began unceremoniously to ply themselves with its contents. This they continued to do in perfect silence for upwards of half an hour. Their flushed cheeks, unsteady hands and glittering eyes then proclaimed that they were in a fit conversational mood. Montmorency addressed his companion thus: 'Dear lambkin, you must be sensible that I am not come here without a reason.'

Rogue: 'Indeed I am, this genuine old antique cognac knows that.'

Montmorency: 'Ah, true, the scent of such fine brandy as

yours is sufficient to draw a corpse from its coffin. But that is not my only reason. I have another.'

'Well, what is it?'

'Why, you know, I suppose, that these staunch upholders of things as they are have got a new recruit who is likely to give us sticklers for freedom some trouble.'

'To be sure I do. Pray, is that the freshest news you've got to tell me?'

'It is both the freshest and the most important, but I have a comment of my own appended to it which is this. This Sydney, or Kidney, or whatever you call him, must be got rid of.'

'The note is as stale as the text; every wise man knows that.'

'Well, but how is the business to be managed?'

'How! Montmorency, are you such a fool as to ask that question?'

'Yes, but I can answer it likewise, the knife, the assassin's knife, must be put into requisition.'

'Of course.'

'Will you undertake the affair or shall I?'

'You may. My heart and hand shall be engaged in another quarter.'

'Eh? What game is the blood-sucker flying at now?'

'At what some men would call lofty game, but what I consider it rather a degradation than otherwise to pursue. The Marquis of Douro before many months shall lie a dead man never to be raised again.'

'The Marquis of Douro? But gentle Alick, how will you get at him without risk to yourself?'

'Fear nothing! I have laid my plans and, now I think on it, you may as well dispose of your man at the same time and in the same manner – that is if you possess sufficient courage to

64

take and break oaths terrible enough to shake Earth to her foundations!'

'Ha! Ha! Ha! When did my courage ever fail in the service of Satan? I should glory to discover some crime of a blacker dye than ever was perpetrated by man before. Speak out then quickly, and let us have done with enigmas.'

'Come this way a little, while I instruct you in your trade, for I should not much like the idea of being overheard. It would be more than my head is worth.'

The two worthy associates then stepped out onto a balcony. There they continued walking about and conversing in earnest undertones until the twilight, for it was now long after sunset, had faded into darkness. A keen, chilly wind, creeping over the bosom of the Guadiana which flowed near, at last compelled them to re-enter the room. They seated themselves again at the table, and commenced a second attack on the half-emptied brandy cask. During the space of three hours they drained it incessantly, but at the end of that period Montmorency, putting in his glass for the sixty-fifth time, brought it up dry. He then rose, cursed the shallowness of all kegs, tubs, casks, butts and barrels, told Rogue that he was a miserly hound or he would send for another supply, and with sundry incomprehensible oaths and interjections staggered out of the apartment.

Lord Ellrington left it shortly after likewise. His gait, however, was still steady and equable. He proceeded to the entrance hall, summoned his carriage and, jumping in, commanded his coachman to drive to the House of Commons. On his arrival there, this extraordinary man delivered a speech which for brilliancy of effect, strength of declamation, and power of appeal has never been surpassed, and but seldom equalled. By his manner no one could have discovered that he was intoxicated. It was graceful, dignified and tranquil, but his eye, as usual, revealed the secret. The wild, wandering, restless light, the intensity of brightness which filled it, imparted an almost maniacal expression to every feature.

Dawn was glimmering in the eastern heavens before he returned home and, before he laid his aching and throbbing head on an unquiet pillow, the rising sun beamed again on the green ocean. For the present I shall leave him in the enjoyment of a brief interval of repose and advert to the other personages of my tale.

7

By this time Sydney was become a confirmed admirer of Lady Julia Wellesley. Restless and lovesick, he haunted the house where she resided, or wandered about his own apartments in melancholy and listless abstraction, carefully weighing his grounds for hope or despair, sometimes hoping that the balance inclined to one side, and sometimes fearing that it leant to the other. This adjustment of accounts indeed was rendered exceedingly puzzling by the apparent caprice of the fair lady's manner. Occasionally she would treat him with a degree of confidence and tenderness that raised his spirits to the very highest pitch, and then again, she would assume an air of such distant and chilling reserve as nearly compelled him to abandon all hope and give himself up a prey to utter wretchedness. In this fluctuating state of his feelings, he found it impossible to attend with due regularity to business. Often when he sat down to meditate a speech or concoct some political pamphlet, his thoughts would perversely deviate from the subject, and entangle him in deep reflection on Lady Julia's last smile or frown, turn of the head, glance of the eye, etc.

This state of mind could not long remain concealed from the penetrating eye of his friend the Marquis and, accordingly, one evening when they were sitting together, Sydney happening to return an irrelevant answer to some question which had been propounded to him, he broke the ice by saying, 'Ned, what has been the matter with you lately? I fancy some part either of your mental or corporeal system must be out of order for you cannot return a decent answer to a civil question.'

Ned made an abortive attempt at a laugh as he replied that he was perfectly well both internally and externally.

'I see,' said the Marquis, 'that you will not speak the truth and therefore I must do it for you. To be plain then, you are in love!' Sydney started, but his examiner went on. 'And I know likewise who has stolen your heart. It is no other than my cousin Julia. Now answer me truly, Ned, is it not so?'

After a moment's pause he answered, 'My lord, I will not deny what your sagacity has discovered. I do love that lady with all my heart, mind and soul, and I even presume to hope that my affection is not wholly unrequited.'

'If Julia has given you any reason for that hope, she has acted like a fool, because (I may as well tell you how matters stand at once, that you may know how to conduct yourself) she can never be your wife.'

'My lord! How? What is it you mean?'

'Simply what I say. She cannot be married to you because she has been long promised to another.'

'Then am I entirely to give up hope – to resign myself for ever to despair?'

'No, Edward, but you must instantly renounce every idea of possessing her, and then endeavour to bear up against the disappointment like a man.'

'I cannot give her up!' said Sydney in a tone of agony. The Marquis looked at him with compassion but did not speak. A long silence followed, which he at last broke by saying: 'Who, my lord, is her destined husband?'

'Sir James Avon, the gentleman who was with me when I first met you, and Julia's partner at the ball in Sulorac Street.'

'Wretch!' exclaimed Sydney. 'When I first saw him I conceived a horror and detestation of his whole person and appearance! Does your cousin love the insignificant puppy?'

'No, I do not think she has the least regard for him.'

'Then who dares to say that she will marry him?'

'Her father, Edward, the Marquis of Wellesley. Sir James is already possessed of large property and is besides heir apparent to his uncle the Earl of Cathcart's title and estates. Julia and he were betrothed to each other at a very early age, and their nuptials are to be celebrated as soon as her father can arrive from England, whence he is now on his way to this country.'

'But, my lord, could you sanction such an alliance with your approbation?'

'No, yet I would not advise you to cherish hopes which are certain to end in bitter disappointment. Had you been of high birth and immense fortune, perhaps my uncle might in time have been induced to retract his promise to Sir James, whom I consider wholly unworthy of Julia, and to consent that she should be united with you. As it is I think there isn't the slightest chance of your success.'

'Would to God,' exclaimed Sydney, 'that I could discover my parents! The tokens I possess seem to intimate that their rank was not obscure. Then – but I dare not encourage the idea, it is impossible, utterly impossible. Oh, that I might die on the spot, I have lost all enjoyment and all pleasure in life!' He dropped his face on his hands and groaned deeply.

The Marquis, much moved, bent over him with tenderness and taking his hand said, 'Dear Edward, do not quite despair. My cousin, I am certain, loves you, and I am as certain that she despises your rival. Julia is a girl of sense and spirit, and will not marry the object of her contempt. Besides my opinion is of some weight with her, and all the influence I posses shall be exerted in your behalf.'

'My lord! I thank you from my heart! From my inmost soul I thank you! Noble generous friend, in what manner can I best testify my gratitude?'

'By composing yourself and making use of the fine sense Nature has granted you. Now goodbye and recollect to keep up your spirits.' He then took leave with a cordial pressure of the hand and one of *his* smiles.

I have said before that Waterloo Palace is built on the summit of a lofty precipice which sinks almost perpendicularly down to the sea, from which it is separated only by a narrow slip of sand. To this place Sydney repaired shortly after the Marquis left him, and continued walking on the little beach until sunset, soothed by the hollow murmur of the waves as they broke in long shining ridges at his feet, and the harmonious whisper of the trees whose branches waved a hundred feet above him. Verdopolis lay far west. Its stately towers and turrets shone like fairy buildings of gold. Ships crowded the distant harbour. Magnificent barges and yachts were skimming with spread sails over its deep blue bosom, while the oar-chant of the rowers and the louder voice of commerce came with such distinctness through the clear calm atmosphere that the words they uttered might have been heard by an attentive listener. The gentle influence of the scene and hour were not lost on Sydney's mind. They seemed to fall with a balmy, soothing power on his heart, and in some measure dispelled the tormenting reflections which filled it. Still he could think but of one subject: of Julia, her beauty, her goodness. And the agonising thought that she could never be his continued to recur at intervals with fearful and nearly overwhelming violence. Whilst he was in this state of mind, a strain of music suddenly swelled high above him. He listened. A sweet soft voice soon mingled with the sound, and the song which follows floated through the sky in almost angelic accents.

O wind that over the ocean
    Comes wafted from the west
And fans with gentle motion
    The deep's unquiet breast,

Say, hast thou passed a stately ship
    On the broad and boundless sea?
Did the crimson flag of England float
    From her main-mast gallantly?

Did the pleasant sound of singing
    Rise from her gentle gale?
Were harps in concert ringing
    With the trumpet's hollow wail?

And as she breasted the waters blue
    And severed the mighty main,
Didst thou see upon her lordly deck
    Some prince or noble's train?

Was snowy plumage streaming?
    Were rich robes waving free?
Were jewels brightly beaming
    'Neath a purple canopy?

Spirit of the western breeze,
Silent sweeper of the seas,
If thou hast seen that gallant ship
Sailing the unfathomed deep,
Soon my doom shall sealed be,
Fixed my future destiny.
Soon in saddest, wildest woe

I shall mourn my hapless love.
Yes 'ere heaven's crescent bow
Shall light again this cedar grove,
I shall stand a weeping bride
At the altar's hallowed side.
But though lost to me for ever,
Worshipped, cherished of my heart,
I can still forget thee never,
Though on earth we part.
Loved one, we may meet again
In a land uncursed by pain.

Sydney, who had begun to ascend the precipice by a winding path on hearing the first well-known tones, now entered the grove where the fair, inspired one was singing. He rushed forward and threw himself at her feet. In blushing and beautiful embarrassment she attempted to withdraw, but so earnestly did he entreat her to remain an instant if she would not at once break his heart, that she was at length forced in a manner to comply. Then, with all the eloquence that love and despair could suggest, he poured out his long-restrained passion. She listened with tears and trembling for some time. After he had ceased, her emotion would not permit her to frame an answer, but at length she said in a faltering voice, 'This stroke which I have so long dreaded has at length fallen upon me. Sydney, I cannot give you any hope. My father is stern and inexorable; he would rather see me in my grave then married to a nameless, untitled stranger. Yet if the assurance that I love you, that I will never be the wife of another if I cannot be yours, will give you any comfort, accept it.' Without waiting for a reply she turned, glided from the grove and disappeared.

Sydney's heart beat with a mixture of joy and sorrow as he again paced the lonely seashore. He was rejoiced at the promise of faithfulness and the declaration of affection which he had just received, and saddened at the mournful certainty that her father's consent to his union with Lady Julia could never be obtained. While he was thus lost in deep meditation the sound of approaching footsteps startled him from his reverie. He looked up. The figure of a tall man in military uniform, dimly visible by the waning light, stood before him. For a moment he regarded him in profound silence. Sydney strove to discern his features, but the shadow of his plumed hat, aided by the position in which he stood against a faintly illumined horizon, forbade this. In a deep and low voice he said, 'Is this his son, or his spirit? Has the grave received permission to give up its dead or has Nature's hand so exactly moulded the child's features into the father's likeness?'

'Sir,' said Sydney, 'who and what are you that hold such mysterious language?'

'Edward Sydney,' replied the stranger, 'ascertain your own name and lineage before you enquire into those of others.'

'That I would give the world to do, but alas it is impossible.'

'It is not impossible.'

'How? Can you assist me in the search?'

'I both can and will. Return to this place at this hour three weeks hence. Then put yourself implicitly under my guidance and I will soon place a coronet on your brow. Farewell.'

The stranger walked slowly away. Sydney gazed intently after him, but the deepening night and the clustered rocks soon concealed his majestic form.

8

A stranger passing through the streets of Verdopolis on the morning of 9th June 1833, might easily have perceived that some heavy cloud, some threatened explosion, hung over its devoted inhabitants. Business seemed wholly neglected. The clanking mills were silent. Sluggish wreaths of smoke unenlivened by flame rose from the forsaken furnaces. The shops indeed were open, but no customer appeared at their counters, except when some solitary individual stepped into a hardware shop to purchase a gun, sword or some other weapon of defence. Numerous groups lounged in the streets, all conversing earnestly and under their breath on some apparently important topic. Files of soldiers were likewise observable drawn out in all the principal streets. These seemed to be regarded by the populace with peculiar animosity. Many a fierce eye and dark brow scowled defiance on them as they stood resting on their arms, but no overt act of intimidation had been yet attempted. Before Bravey's Hotel a vast crowd was assembled, yet no loud exclamation of mirth or anger rose from it, only a dull, incessant and most ominous murmur. The Rotunda contained a more select company; still dissatisfaction and sullen gloom alike brooded over every countenance.

My reader will doubtless enquire the reason of all this. I will satisfy his curiosity in a few words. About two months previous to the commencement of this chapter, and a month subsequent to the conclusion of the last, Lord Ellrington, Mr Montmorency, Mr Sydney, the Duke of Wellington and the Marquis of Douro had suddenly and unaccountably disappeared. Search had been made after them in vain. Messengers had been dispatched in all directions. Thousands of miles had been traversed without success. In short every means both possible and impossible had been employed to discover them, but to no purpose. Rumours then began to spread through the city. The lower classes, who idolised Lord Ellrington, asserted that he and Mr Montmorency had been treacherously entrapped by the government; that they had been either murdered or imprisoned by it; and some of the most zealous openly urged their copatriots to revenge their wrongs. The higher orders, on the contrary, maintained that foul play was on the side of the demagogues. That the Duke, the Marquis and Sydney were the victims of some horrid and concealed plot, and that it was the duty of government to pursue a strict enquiry until some definite clue to the whole affair should be discovered. Parliament, in the meantime, met every night, but their irregular and stormy debates, far from soothing the general excitement, only served to add fresh fuel to a fire whose fierceness already seemed to threaten a universal conflagration.

In this state of affairs a grand council was summoned by their majesties Alexander, William and John.[30] The result of their deliberations was a resolution to ask Crashie's[31] advice, and to be determined by his words. Accordingly deputies to the number of one hundred were selected for this purpose, and the 9th June was appointed for their visit to the Tower of All Nations. On the morning of this day they had proceeded thither, and now all Verdopolis waited in sullen yet impatient silence for the consequences of their application.

After the lapse of four tedious hours, the brazen gates on the north side unfolded and the train issued forth. Thousands immediately crowded round them, eagerly enquiring what council the great patriarch had given. They returned no answer, but with hurried steps and visages of blank dismay proceeded to the hall where the kings and nobles were deliberating. Alexander rose as they entered.

'Gentlemen,' said he, 'what are Our Father's commands? Deliver them that we may hasten to obey.'

Gravey,[32] who had headed the deputation, stepped forward. 'I fear,' he answered, 'that the hour of our city's destruction is come. We have sought the great Crashie in his sanctuary, but he is also departed. The light which shone round him is vanished, his throne and shrine are empty, and now we are indeed forsaken.'

There was a pause. Horror seemed to have fallen on all. Alexander folded his arms as if in despair. William sternly knit his brows, and John instinctively grasped the sword which hung at his side. This silence, however, was not of long duration. The three monarchs simultaneously rose, dissolved the council, and adjourned to the Parliament House. Here they caused the disastrous intelligence they had just received to be announced. Its effect was similar to that which had been produced on the council. A sense of desertion, a cold dreary chill struck to every heart.

When the first terrible impression had in some measure passed off, a few members rose and pointed out what appeared to them the most probable means of preventing a rising in the city when the news should spread, but all was so lame, so vague, and so unsatisfactory that no decisive conclusion could be arrived at. While they were thus employed, a loud but distant shout, followed by a sound of the discharge of musketry, announced that the evil they sought to prevent had already taken place. Upwards of twenty thousand extraordinary copies of the *Young Men's Intelligencer*, communicating the event, had in three hours' time been struck off and circulated through Verdopolis. Dismay, as usual, was the first feeling which prevailed but, as this subsided, rage and suspicion took its place.

The peasantry, instigated by their ambitious leaders, Naughty, Ned Laury,[33] etc., declared that Crashie's disappearance was merely a pretence to blind them and distract their attention from the main point of Rogue's assassination. They now asserted likewise that he was imprisoned in the vast dungeons beneath the Tower of All Nations. An immense crowd assembled round it, which, at the word of command, formed itself into squares, files, battalions, etc., etc., with the accuracy of a well-disciplined army. Through these armed and ferocious-looking ranks, Naughty passed to and fro, exhorting them, with that rude eloquence which was best calculated to produce the desired effect, to stand firm and to flinch neither before soldiers nor fiends. They answered with loud shouts, crying out that they wanted nothing but an opportunity and they would tear every redcoat in Verdopolis to atoms.

'Bravo! Then, my rare souls,' exclaimed Naughty, 'make a rush to the north gates and see whether they will stand your bludgeons. We'll soon have him amongst us again.'

With a simultaneous yell, the mob poured off to the point indicated. A terrific attack now commenced on the brazen doors. They groaned and trembled under the storm, but remained immovable. At this juncture of affairs a voice from the outskirts of the assaulting party cried out that the soldiers were approaching. 'Let them come. We fear them not,' thundered a thousand tongues at once.

The words were scarcely uttered before a regiment of cavalry, headed by Colonel Grenville, galloped into the square.

'Countrymen!' he exclaimed, rising in his stirrups. 'What frightful madness has seized you? Do you know that you are now committing an act of the blackest sacrilege? Back, I say, or this instant my band shall fire on you.'

He was answered by a peal of contemptuous laughter. The signal was then given, and the regiment fired. About twenty men were wounded and one or two killed by this discharge. The mob, instead of being dismayed, were only still more infuriated. They turned from the tower and began to surround Colonel Grenville.

A horrible struggle now ensued. Both sides fought desperately. The yells of onset and the shouts of partial victory rose mingled with the groans of the wounded and dying. But, notwithstanding the superior discipline of the military, they would soon have been overpowered by almost countless numbers had not a fresh reinforcement, headed by John Ross[34] himself, arrived. He charged the dense gathering multitude with irresistible impetuosity. Naughty, in vain, urged them onwards. In vain, like an enraged demon, he sprung from line to line, calling down fearful curses, and imprecating vengeance on the heads of those who fled. By degrees the living mass melted. Thousands sought safety in flight, and the few who remained were cut to pieces. Their leader at length stood alone in the square environed by the dead, the dying, and his enemies. With white hair streaming from his unbonneted head, with eyes glaring like coals of fire, he still continued brandishing a leaden club, and dilating his gigantic form to its utmost, in hoarse and frantic voice calling on the renegades to return. Ross, who admired his courage, generously forbade the soldiers to fire on him. It was not, however, without the utmost difficulty that he was taken alive, and when this was effected, it was found necessary instantly to convey him to prison lest he should escape.

In a few hours the city, which had been a scene of such

tremendous tumult, sunk to almost unbroken silence. Every street seemed deserted. The shutters of the shops and houses were closed. The heaps of slaughtered bodies which lay round the tower were removed. A shower had washed all traces of blood from the pavement and in short, not a vestige of the recent conflict remained, save some companies of soldiers who still guarded the streets. In this tranquil state of affairs night came on gloriously and peacefully.

The sun withdrew its huge blood-red disk. Not a solitary cloud traversed heaven, not a speck defaced its ethereal clearness when the round full moon shone above the long eastern hills.

Calm as the city looked, while it lay under that soft sky bathed in tender lustre, many an aching heart beat within its proud walls; many a sorrow-laden bosom refused the offered balm of repose. Lady Julia Wellesley sat weeping at her casement, gazing with tearful eyes over the dark sea, and almost wishing herself buried in the unsounded waters which rolled far beneath. Her father had arrived two months since. She had candidly declared to him her attachment to Sydney, and on her knees besought him not to compel her to a union with Sir James Avon. But the Marquis, though he loved his daughter, was of a stern and obstinate cast of mind. He had long set his heart on this marriage as the most eligible settlement in life he could provide for her. Besides, Sir James possessed his promise, and that he determined not to break or rescind for the caprice of a foolish, whimsical girl.

This night, therefore, had been appointed for their marriage, which was to take place at eleven o'clock in the private chapel belonging to Waterloo Palace, where the Marquis resided during his stay in Verdopolis. It was now nine, Julia had just retired to her apartment after a last but ineffectual attempt to shake her father's resolution by prayers, tears and entreaties. This room overlooked the cedar grove where Sydney had revealed his love, and received her final farewell. In an agony of despair she threw herself on a couch by the window, wept until tears refused any longer to relieve the weight of grief which lay cold and heavy at her heart, and then fixed her wandering gaze on the billows which glittered and flashed in moonlight through the blackening boughs without. For a long time nothing appeared but the ever-following waves. Not a lonely fishing boat enlivened the vast monotonous expanse. But at last a dim white sail appeared gleaming far to westward. On it came, rapid and silent as a bird. Julia watched its gliding progress to the shore until tall intervening rocks hid it from her sight. Again she relapsed into a state of apathetic despondency. The temporary interest which this little bark had excited vanished with its object. She laid her head on her hand and continued motionless in that position until roused by a rap at the door.

'Come in,' said she faintly.

A maid servant entered with candles, and, depositing them on the table, said, 'Madam, will you be pleased to dress now. It wants a little more than an hour of the time.'

'I am ready, Clara,' she replied, rising from her seat.

The increased light now served to display the bridal preparations which lay around. Ornaments of diamond and strings of pearl glittered on the toilet. A splendid white satin dress was carefully hung on a chair-back, while a wreath of orange flowers, a little golden ring and the pearl crescent worn by our ladies were placed on the table near.

In passive silence Lady Julia permitted her thick dark tresses to be curled, braided and adorned with the jewels appropriated for that purpose. Unresistingly she suffered the maid to array her in her rich robes, place the snowy pearls round her neck, the diamond bracelets on her wrists, to adorn her head with the nuptial garland, and her brow with the pale crescent. When all was concluded she sank back as if exhausted, and burst into a flood of bitter tears.

'Oh do not cry, my lady,' said Clara. 'You will spoil your beautiful dress.'

'Ah, Clara, if that was all I had to care for, I should be happy – most happy.'

Clara made no answer but thought it was very strange that a lady should be so sorrowful just before she was going to be married. Eleven o'clock at length arrived. As it struck, the Marquis of Wellesley entered his daughter's apartment.

'Julia,' said he, kindly taking her hand, 'Sir James is come, and everything is now ready. Do, my dear girl, strive to meet him with a less mournful countenance.'

'Father, I cannot. My heart is breaking. I feel that I shall die this night if you proceed to enforce your cruel commands.'

'Silence, self-willed and disobedient child! I, who have a right to compel, condescend to entreat – and you dare to answer me thus.'

'O, I will not marry him! I will not break my faith to poor lost Edward, not if the rack were to be the punishment of my constancy!'

Lady Julia uttered this exclamation in frenzied and almost maniacal accents. The Marquis seemed moved by her deep distress, but, instantly recovering himself, he answered, 'These romantic airs lose their effect upon me. What presumption inspires you to utter the name of that beggarly foundling in my ears again?' She answered only by sobs. 'Rise,' he continued, 'and follow me directly. I have already humoured your caprice too long.'

He quitted the room and she, not daring to resist, followed in silence. They proceeded down the great staircase to the entrance hall, and from thence through a long passage which led to the private chapel. This was a grand but gloomy edifice in the Gothic style of architecture. The scene which it presented that night might have formed a fit subject for a painter. Tall, clustering pillars rose to the roof, partly illuminated by the faint torchlight, and partly by the still fainter moonbeams which, falling through arched windows of stained glass, chequered the pavement with the soft reflection of their gorgeous tints. Two lighted wax tapers by the high altar threw a dazzling breadth of light on the group which stood near, consisting of the fair, mourning bride, the dandy, dapper bridegroom, the Marquis with his stern yet noble countenance, and the venerable, silver-haired chaplain. This breadth, however, was cast only over a limited space. The termination of the long aisle was lost in total darkness, unbroken even by the moon, for no window there admitted its rays. Impenetrable obscurity also involved the roof which towered high above the influence of the few dim lamps burning below.

For a short time after Lady Julia and her father had entered, there was a profound silence. But soon Mr Rundell's deep mellow voice thrilled through the echoing cloisters, which repeated his words in hollower tones as he pronounced the introductory part of the marriage ceremony.

Sir James had solemnly plighted his troth before heaven, had sworn to love, honour and cherish his wife for ever, and now it became Julia's turn to utter her portion of the awful oath. 'Wilt thou,' said the chaplain, 'wilt thou take this man for thy wedded husband?'

Her cheek turned deadly pale, but her eye flashed heroic fire as she answered, 'I will – not.'

There was a pause. Mr Rundell closed his book. Sir James gasped and looked stupefied. The Marquis bit his lip until the blood sprang, but no one spoke. Before long, however, this dread stillness was interrupted by a sound like the tread of footsteps approaching up the darkened aisle. Presently, faintly defined figures became visible, and, in another instant, Lady Julia was clasped in the arms of her recovered Sydney. Her father laid his hand on his sword, but before he could draw it his thoughts were diverted into another channel by the appearance of the Duke of Wellington and the Marquis of Douro.

'Brother,' said the former advancing, and bestowing on him a fraternal embrace, 'before I bid you welcome to the shores of Africa let me hear you promise that my pretty niece shall have her own way in the choice of a husband.'

'Arthur,' said he, 'do you know what you are asking? She has fixed her heart on a foundling – a man without birth, rank, title and almost without fortune.'

'No, Richard, you are totally mistaken. I have discovered his origin, and let me assure you that a union with him will rather elevate than debase your daughter.'

'Surely he has deceived you?'

'That is impossible. But let us leave this gloomy chapel and retire to some place more suited to conversation, where I will explain the whole mystery to your satisfaction.'

'I am ready to attend you, yet I greatly doubt whether you will be able to remove my scruples.'

'We shall see. Come, Arthur, follow with poor Jemmy, and you, Edward, take charge of Lady Julia.'

The party then returned to the palace, where they found Lord Ellrington and Mr Montmorency. Here I will leave them engaged in an éclaircissement, and, in the meantime, proceed to relate the whole affair my own way, beginning with the disappearance of the Marquis of Douro, Lord Ellrington and Mr Montmorency, which my readers will find was a business perfectly distinct from that of the Duke and Mr Sydney. This relation, however, ought not to come in at the end of a chapter; therefore, I will now commence a new one.

9

At a distance of nearly six hundred miles from the continent of Africa, there lies an island called the Philosopher's Island. It is extensive but barren, being covered principally with heath and forests. Through the middle runs a ridge of dark wild hills, which are known by the name of the Gordale Mountains. Embosomed in these is a vast and deep valley where the only building on the island stands. This has the appearance of a strongly fortified castle, being flanked by four turreted towers, and surrounded by thick stone ramparts. But it is in reality a sort of college or university for the instruction of the rising generation. Here the most learned philosophers in the world have their residence, and to this place all the noble youth of Verdopolis are sent for their education.

There has lately been formed amongst the professors and tutors of the university a secret society of which many of the principal characters in our city are members. This association is said to have dived deeply into the mysteries of Nature, and to have revealed many of her hidden and unthought-of secrets. On the night of 6th of April 1833, a meeting of its members was suddenly summoned by the president. They are said to possess the power of passing with supernatural rapidity from one place to another but, however this may be, many of them who were in Africa on the morning of that day, before midnight stood on the shores of the Philosopher's Island. The place of their assembling suited well with their mysterious character. It was a dark subterraneous vault, situated under the castle or college. Iron lamps, suspended from the low arched roof, served to shed a dim glimmer on the numerous masked and black-robed figures who appeared beneath, gliding with a spirit-like tread through the surrounding gloom. Not a step or voice was heard, as they slowly arranged themselves in a half-circle before a lofty throne, which stood in the centre of the vault, on which sat an aged man[35] who seemed to be more than a hundred years old. He was of kingly stature; his forehead was bald, but a long beard as white as snow flowed down lower than his girdle. In his right hand he held a sort of sceptre, and a golden circlet glittered among his grey venerable locks.

'Children,' he began in a deep and awful tone while all his disciples bowed reverently before him, 'I have called you to my presence this night on a melancholy and mournful occasion. You know that, after long and painful research, after diving into the profound and troubled depths of the sea, after seeking earth's concealed and unknown treasures, after nightly watching and daily wandering, I at last succeeded in compounding a fluid, so pure, so refined, so ethereal that one drop of it distilled on our mortal clay penetrated to the soul, freed it from all grosser particles, raised it far above worldly troubles, rendered it capable of enjoying the calm of heaven amid the turmoil of earth, and as with a shield of adamant, for ever warded off the darts of death. Such was my discovery. To you I revealed the secret, to you, my children, from whom I could hide nothing that would benefit you. I taught you at what season to gather the rare herbs whose subtle juice mingled in the celestial liquid, under what conjunction of the planetary signs to speak those mystic words which should draw earth's precious stores from her inmost recesses, and compel ocean to rifle her tomb-dark and silent caverns, where voice never whispered, where sun never beamed. Yes, for your sakes my tongue spoke of the grand and terrible, yet forbidden art, until our world trembled in mid-space. I felt the convulsion. I knew that if longer I had spoken or you had listened there would have been ruin in the sky, and I paused, but it was too late. Those high and unseen spirits to whom even I, potent as I am among men, must yield, had heard me. Dread indignation awoke in their mighty bosoms. They stooped from their four-fold thrones and smote my presumption with a curse. Yes, when I turned to sprinkle on your heads that water of life, that divine nectar, I saw that it was changed. A black and bloody slime stagnated in the crystal vessel where before liquid transparency had shone. A fetid odour like the exhalations of hell rose from it instead of ambrosial perfumes. I knew, too, that a change had passed over its nature as well as its appearance. Now, instead of dispensing immortality and holy delight, it would bring the horrors, the darkness of inevitable death, the fearful agony of tormented fiends. I was thunderstruck, and to increase my misery came the tremendous consciousness that I had brought this new curse on my fellow creatures. I had made you the confidants of a secret which you might hereafter wrest to your own destruction, or that of others. To prevent this I devised an oath which few may take and live. I made you swear by names and things ineffable, thrice-holy, that you would never practise the fatal knowledge which had been imparted to you, that you would never make use of this infernal draught, even though the murderer by its aid could not possibly be amenable to an earthly tribunal. As one by one you uttered the oath, these heavy arches and this solid pavement rocked as if a troubling earthquake had been heaving its hot billows underneath. Then all who swore signed their names in letters of blood to this parchment scroll, but you did so unknowing that if any among you should become perjured his name would instantly be transformed from blood to glowing fire: every night I examined the roll, and the last evening, while

I was doing so, a sudden blighting flame blazed over the withered parchment and revealed that Alexander, Lord Ellrington had dared my inexorable wrath.'

The magician paused. A shudder ran through his terrified disciples, but no one ventured to utter a word. He went on: 'I summoned my familiar spirit. I bade him bring the vile assassin and his accomplices (if he had any) and his victim before me, should they be at the other extremity of the globe. What was my sorrow, my soul-rending grief, when I recognised in the murdered corpse my beloved and favourite disciple Arthur, Marquis of Douro.'

He paused again and made a mystic sign with his sceptre. An iron door immediately unfolded, and six dark figures, bearing a bier covered with a white sheet, entered. Two others followed, one of whom conducted Lord Ellrington bound in chains, and the other Mr Montmorency, who was likewise fettered. The bier was deposited before the throne and the criminals placed beside it.

'Remove the covering,' said the magician in a low voice.

It was done, and the Marquis's majestic form became visible, stretched in the immovable rigidity of death. A cold marble paleness was settled on his sunk but still noble features. The rich close curls had fallen back from his forehead and displayed all its snow-white dazzling breadth. His eyes were closed. The proud yet generous spirit which once shone in them was now extinct. Sealed lids and dark fringing lashes now concealed their brilliancy. Lord Ellrington and Mr Montmorency looked on the corpse without any apparent emotion. The countenance of the former was firm and intrepid. That of the latter had a mixture of insolent assurance.

'Bold miscreant,' began their stern judge addressing Lord

Ellrington. 'Can you gaze unmoved on that fair flower which your machinations have so untimely cut off?'

'I can!' replied Rogue, 'because my conscience approves the deed; that young man was my deadly enemy. Nature teaches us to destroy those whom we hate. I listened to her dictates and he died.'

'And dost thou hearken only to the ever-erring voice of thy unrestrained passions?'

'What better guide can I look up to? The brute which is devoid of reason knows by instinct that the creature who has offended him is a legitimate object on which to wreak his vengeance.'

'And thou, on whom the deity has bestowed the glorious gift of a soul, placest thyself on a level with the beast that perisheth.'

'We do not understand the hypocritical jargon of superstition,' interrupted Montmorency, 'speak plainly, old gentleman, and we will answer civilly.'

The magician cast on him a withering glance of scorn and, turning to Rogue, he proceeded, 'I perceive that thou hast chosen a worthy associate in this daring crime, but think not that the sword of justice can be blunted by insolence. The cup which my Arthur drank shall be returned with ten-fold bitterness to your own perjured lips.'

'Do your worst, driveling dotard,' answered he, with a cold smile. 'I have tried life and found it anything but a bed of roses. The pains of death will be short though perhaps sharp, and as for a hereafter, the illusion of heaven and the bugbear of hell form no part of my creed. A sound, unbroken and eternal sleep is the worst I have to anticipate.'

'Aye Rogue, that's spoken like a man,' said Montmorency. 'Come, Long-beard, give us this same nightcap of yours quickly, that we may go to bed. It's cursedly cold standing in this damp cellar.'

The magician again signed. The iron door opened, and one of the shadowy forms which had before appeared entered bearing a vessel filled with some substance that had the appearance of semi-coagulated blood. He placed it in his master's hands and departed. Immediately thick wreaths of vapour began to rise from the pavement and, gradually forming themselves into a dense cloud, soon concealed the judge, the criminals, and the bier from sight.

A brief but profound silence followed, which was dissipated by a terrific shriek, almost loud enough to have rent the surrounding veil asunder. A voice murmured, 'Is it over?'

'No, assassin,' was the stern reply, 'it is but begun.'

Another period of silence followed, succeeded by a louder and longer scream. Shrieks and yells now followed without intermission. For upwards of half an hour the horrible struggle continued, and then these thrilling expressions of agony by degrees subsided into ghastly groans and low dying sobs that made the flesh of the listeners creep on their bones.

All again sank to perfect stillness. The clouds slowly rolled away, revealing as they disappeared the dead bodies of Lord Ellrington and Mr Montmorency. Torture had wrung and distorted their countenances into the most fearful semblance that death can assume. Drops of cold sweat, elicited by the sufferings they had endured, hung on their livid foreheads and damped their writhen features. With eyes starting from their sockets and closely clenched hands they yet appeared to upbraid that justice which had thus commended the poisoned chalice to their lips.

'Children,' exclaimed the unrelenting magician, 'behold the victims of my justly aroused wrath. Behold and tremble.'

The last command was unnecessary. A universal shuddering had seized on every spectator. Seeing that this dreadful example had now produced the desired effect, he permitted them all to retire. They gladly availed themselves of this licence and in a few minutes he was left alone with the three corpses. In this undesirable company I must leave him for the present and see what my hero My Sydney has been about in the meantime.

Edward punctually kept his assignation with the mysterious stranger. Long before the appointed hour he repaired to the lonely sea beach. The night formed a strange contrast with that on which he had last visited the spot. Heavy and dark clouds shrouded all the moonless sky. An unfelt but distinctly heard wind moaned faintly through the air and over the sea which swelled in long low waves, breaking on the shore with a solemn and almost harmonious sound. Verdopolis was now invisible; nothing could be seen in that direction but a dazzling galaxy of a thousand stars increased to the magnitude of suns by the thick hazy atmosphere through which they quivered and trembled, bright and lustrous as the genuine lamps of heaven. Softly the city's subdued voice mingled with the dull rushing of the ocean. No sharper or louder sound interrupted the perfect unison of their blended notes.

Sydney, in other circumstances, might have listened to the monotonous yet soothing strain with pleasure had not his faculties been absorbed by the single yet all-important thought, the fondly cherished hope, that he was this night about to receive information which would enable him to demand Lady Julia of her father with some chance, however remote, of success. With burning impatience he trod the yielding sand, pausing every instant to listen for the sound of approaching footsteps, and eagerly striving to pierce the impenetrable night in search of his promised guide. He looked and listened for a length of time in vain: no tread, however faint, was audible; no form, however dim, apparent.

'He has deceived me,' said he bitterly, 'the man is an imposter. I was a fool to come.'

'You would have been a greater fool had you stayed away,' said someone close at hand.

He turned hastily. A tall figure stood close behind him. 'Who and what are you?' exclaimed Sydney, a little startled at the suddenness of the apparition.

'Do you not know me, Edward?' he replied.

'I do,' answered our hero, now recognising the voice as that of his unknown friend. 'You see I have kept the tryst faithfully, and I hope you will repay the confidence which I have reposed in you, an utter stranger, by an immediate and unreserved communication of all you know respecting my birth and origin.'

'You speak boldly, my lad,' replied the mysterious incognito, 'but I shall have to tax this confidence you boast of a little higher before either that can be rewarded, or your curiosity satisfied. You must take a short voyage of some hundreds of miles with me in a small vessel I have at no great distance.'

'What do you mean, sir?' said Sydney doubtingly.

'Just what I say, Neddy. Will you go and win a coronet, or will you remain and lose one?'

'You proposal is sudden. It requires time for consideration.'

'I will allow you five minutes to decide, and if you refuse my offer then – why, I'll carry you off by main force.'

As he uttered these words Sydney thought that his voice strongly resembled the Marquis of Douro's. It had the same full melody of sound, only the undertones were rather deeper. Struck with this idea he said, 'Have I not seen you before, sir?'

'To be sure. It is scarcely a month since we met on this very spot.'

'Yes, but previously to that.'

'Probably you may.'

'Probably! I am sure of it. Arthur, speak the truth. It is not your very self to whom I am speaking?'

'Arthur!' said the stranger in a tone which indicated that he was half-amused and half-astonished. 'Tolerably familiar that, my lad. You address me by my Christian name, I suppose, in anticipation of your coming dignity.'

'You appear surprised my lord, but I have often called you Arthur before without the circumstance exciting your astonishment in the least.'

'Have you? It is the first time I knew we were so intimately acquainted as to warrant such a mode of address. Where are your wits flown to Master Edward ? I think you had better call them back.'

'Am I mistaken, is it possible that you are not the Marquis of Douro?'

'The Marquis of Douro!' said the unknown with a good-humoured laugh. 'Assuredly I am no more the Marquis of Douro than I am Lord Charles Wellesley. What made you take so odd a notion into your silly young head?'

'Because your accent and manner of speaking are so exactly similar to his that I thought no two persons could own the same mode of utterance.'

'Hem! You find you were mistaken however. Now come, have you decided whether to go quietly with me or to be forced along?'

'I have not as yet reflected on the subject.'

'Make haste then, five minutes you know is the stipulated time.'

Sydney mused in silence for a short time. Was he to give himself up to the guidance of one respecting whom he was utterly ignorant, one who seemed rather inclined to domineer over him and who might, for anything he as yet knew, be trying to lure him on to destruction under the mask of a frank and candid demeanour? The threat of violence which the stranger had used grated strongly on his mind. He was, as I have before hinted, rather obstinate in disposition, and anything which bore the appearance of force was peculiarly obnoxious to him. Under the influence of these considerations, he was just about to utter a firm negative when a voice like that which he had heard long since at Oakwood Hall came up on the cool sea-breeze, and with thrilling emphasis whispered the single word 'OBEY'. The effect was almost magical. He looked up and said promptly, 'I will go with you this instant.'

'Good,' said the stranger. He then uttered a clear, shrill whistle which, ringing over the ocean, was answered by the same signal from a great distance. Before long the dash of oars became audible; a light appeared gliding towards the shore. As it drew near, a boat could be distinctly seen. It was moored on the little beach. Sydney and his conductor immediately embarked. The word was given, and the little vessel shot swiftly away.

Dawn, clad in dim grey weeds, had now begun to ascend the cloudy heavens as the infant day followed her uncertain footsteps. Those vapours which had so drearily shrouded the night rolled gradually away. A long and intensely brilliant line of amber light now threw the eastern hills forward in dark relief. It increased in radiancy; a clear golden gleam appeared in one part, and, at length, large, shield-like and glorious, the sun looked forth on the wide blue world of waters.

There was now amply sufficient light for Sydney to

scrutinise the form and features of his hitherto almost unseen guide, and this he did carefully. He was, as I have said, tall and apparently about forty years of age. His countenance, though handsome, was more remarkable for its singular striking expression than for the regularity of its features. A Roman nose, and a pair of dark bright falcon eyes infused into it such a degree of stern and searching keenness as would have been rather appalling to anyone who might fall by chance under his piercing eagle glance, but for the redeeming softness of the calm, yet not altogether sweet smile, which generally played round a very finely formed mouth, and the imperturbable placidity of his smooth, ample forehead. It was this contra-diction in the expression of his features, this quiescence of the external man, contrasted with the active energy of that mighty spirit shining deep in the quick sparkling eye, which gave that peculiar air, that *je ne sais quoi*, to his whole countenance, and though it declared at once that his mind and genius were of an infinitely loftier rank than that assigned to the common herd of men, yet a casual spectator, on first beholding him, felt more of admiration than love, and more of fear than either. For the rest, his complexion was dark, almost swarthy; his hair, of a glossy brown colour, was arranged with much elegant negligence; his form was stately and commanding; and his manners possessed much of that ease and dignity which belongs to military officers of high rank.

Sydney, who was absorbed in contemplating the fine person of his guide, did not notice the approach of another vessel until the boat halted close under her bows. The sudden swell which this movement, or rather cessation of movement, occasioned, roused him from his reverie.

'Edward,' said the unknown, 'are you a good climber? We shall have to mount the sides of this ship.'

Our hero, who was not deficient in activity, quickly ascended the hanging rope ladder. His friend followed with equal dexterity, and both then proceeded to the state cabin. On entering this apartment Sydney was surprised to observe a rich crimson velvet canopy overhanging a kind of throne, on which sat a very old man with long white beard and hair. On his visage the purest benevolence was finely blended with more than mortal wisdom; a ring of softly beaming light played round his temples and illumined the atmosphere all round him. Struck by this supernatural appearance, Sydney stood at the door gazing fixedly on him, but his companion advanced and, gracefully dropping on one knee before the ancient of days, said, 'Father, the lost is found. It only remains now to restore him to his hereditary rights.'

'Son, thou hast done well,' replied the awful voice of our patriarch. 'Let the youth approach that I may bestow on him a paternal blessing.'

'Draw near, Edward Sydney, and bend before the divine Crashie.'

Sydney, for a moment, stood fixed and entranced, then, springing forward, he fell prostrate at the foot of the throne. Mingled emotions of awe and joy, an overwhelming sense of the sublime presence in which he stood, and a tide of solemn yet rapturous feelings rushing on at him at once, nearly deprived him of recollection.

'Son, I bless thee,' began the glorious ancient. 'Spirits have watched over thee, or, long before this, thou wouldst have sunk into final and irredeemable obscurity. Now, blessed be the Great God of Nature, thou wilt soon be safely restored to the exalted rank which is due alike to thy birth and mind.'

'And who, mighty Father, are the parents to whom I owe my existence?'

'Thou shall know before many suns are set and risen. In the meantime, rest assured that the hope which thy young heart has so fondly cherished shall suffer no chilling blight from the breath of disappointment.'

After a second profound prostration, Sydney retired with his guide. When they were seated in an adjoining cabin, the latter addressed him thus, 'Edward, I will now tell you my name, which you appear rather anxious to know. I am not the Marquis of Douro whom, during our last night's conference you foolishly enough imagined me to be, but I am that young nobleman's father.'

'The Duke of Wellington?' exclaimed Sydney starting to his feet while, as he recollected the familiar manner in which he had conversed with His Grace, the blood rushed rapidly to his usually pale face, 'I – I – I'm sure I beg Your Grace's pardon for – for – '

'For what?' said the Duke smiling. 'I see you don't know.'

'But indeed I do, and that too well, for my inexcusable flippancy and almost insolence.'

The Duke did not seem to hear him. He made no answer, but kindly taking his hand gazed long and sorrowfully on his youthful features. Large tears at length rose into his dark and now softened eyes. As he felt them trickling from thence to his cheek, he flung Sydney's hand from him and, hastily rising, left the cabin. What, thought Sydney, could have drawn those mementos of human weakness from such a man? It must have been some deep, some long-settled sorrow. Can my father have been related to him? Can he have been his brother? The thought is presumptuous! I am an ambitious fool ever to have conceived such an idea!

After a favourable voyage of six days over a wide and seemingly shoreless sea, land at last appeared, looming far off on the southern horizon. As they drew near, the coast presented a bold and rocky appearance. High black cliffs frowned gloomily over the stormy ocean that roared through their high arches and huge riven clefts, or thundered far below in the subaqueous caverns which a thousand on-rushing waves concealed from mortal eye. Flights of sea-birds whirled incessantly round them, shrieking until the blue element rung again with their hoarse wild clamour. A rocky bay appeared stretching far into the country. Here the vessel cast anchor for the night, and next morning Crashie, the Duke of Wellington and Sydney landed alone, unattended by any of the sailors.

'Now,' said the Duke, whose behaviour towards Edward had been characterised by more than a father's tenderness, 'Now, my boy, in a few hours you will learn the important secret of your birth.'

'How can I learn it in a desolate island?' said he with some surprise, as he glanced at the dark barren hills which encompassed them on every side.

'You should not judge by the eye,' replied His Grace. 'A well-cultivated and thickly peopled country is not always the most productive of romantic incidents.'

'But, my lord, are there any inhabitants in this place? I see no signs of men or houses.'

'There are some, but not many.'

After about an hour's journeying over moors and rocks they entered a gloomy and wide glen surrounded by huge heath-clad mountains, and watered by a rapid river which rushed past with all the impetuosity of a hill-torrent. Slowly they moved on, Crashie's aged limbs refusing to bear him with the swift elastic step of youth. He leant however on the supporting arms of his elder and his younger son, as he affectionately termed the Duke and Sydney, and, thus assisted, continued to advance without any considerable degree of fatigue. On turning one of the many windings in which the sinuous valley wound serpent-like along, they suddenly came in sight of a great castellated building situated in the midst of it and surrounded by a moat and fosse with all the other appurtenances common to such edifices, but instead of a guard of soldiers there appeared a number of young men dressed in students' attire walking on the ramparts.

'This fortification is strangely situated and still more strangely defended,' observed Sydney. 'Who built it, my lord?'

'It is not a fortification but simply a college. You have heard of the Philosopher's Island, I suppose?'

'Frequently.'

'The country in which you now are is it, and that is the university of which the great magician Manfred is president.'

As the Duke communicated this information they reached the drawbridge. A sentinel on the wall above exclaimed, 'Who goes there?'

'Friends of Manfred,' replied Crashie, and the bridge was instantly let down.

As they passed through the court every student who was there knelt reverently down, for they immediately recognised Crashie as well by the majesty of his form and face as by the mysterious light hovering round his head. As they arrived at the gate, and were about to knock for entrance, one of the principal philosophers came up and, prostrating himself at the patriarch's feet, said, 'Father, you seek our great president.'

'I do, son, where is he?'

'He has not entered our gates for more than a week, but during that space of time has watched day and night in the Grove of Tears.'

'What fresh sorrow has summoned him there?' said the Duke.

'A deep and sad one,' replied the philosopher in a peculiar tone and turned hastily away.

'We must seek him where he abides, my children,' continued the patriarch.

They signified their acquiescence by a low inclination of the head, and all three returned slowly towards the glen. After walking about a mile further up, it began to grow much narrower. Woods of dark cypresses now also appeared at the latter extremity, the gloom of whose shadow threw a sort of cloud across their way. As they entered it by a winding path, a more than twilight obscurity surrounded them. The thick black boughs were so closely interwoven that scarcely a ray of sunshine or a streak of blue sky appeared to cheer the melancholy darkness. Now, also, a sound of music came floating from a distance. It was inexpressibly mournful. The tones bore a thrilling solemnity which pierced the souls of the listeners and brought unbidden tears to their eyes. As they approached, the following words were audible, sung by a deep and strong yet not inharmonious voice.

Sound a lament in the halls of his father,
Waken the harp-strings and pour forth a wail,
The caves of the hill the sad echoes will gather,
The chant will be sung by the wandering gale.
Damp lies his corpse in the folds of the shroud
And low to the dust his bright forehead is bowed.

Weep in thy chambers where music is sighing,
Weep in thy palace fair bride of his heart,
Thy love with the worms of corruption is lying,

Thou from his bosom for ever must part.
For ever, for ever, how sad is that word
When by the lone grave of the buried 'tis heard.

Shake from thy tresses the flower-wreath of gladness,
Scatter its bloom to the winds of the sky,
Cover thy brow with a mantle of sadness,
Weep, for thy moment of mourning draws nigh
And leave that bright robe of the youthful and gay
For the grief-darkened weeds of a widow's array.

But longer and louder uplift a shrill wail
For the parent of him who sleeps low with the dead.
His eye shall grow dim and his cheek shall turn pale
And the plumes shall droop low on that proud warrior's head
When he treads the lone isle of the desolate shore,
When he hears that his loved one, his son, is no more.

He fell not in battle, he fell not in war
Where conquest and carnage have followed his might.
No, suddenly, silently, vanished his star,
At noonday fell on him the darkness of night.
A murderer's voice bade his spirit depart,
The hand of a traitor brought death to his heart.

O, why was the morn of his young being clouded
By darkness so solemn, by horror so deep?
And why was that fair form, all fettered and shrouded,
So early laid down in its long dreamless sleep?
What hand can dispel that dense, shadowy gloom
Which hides from our vision the volume of doom?

As this ominous strain ended, the party cleared the wood and entered a sort of open glade, which, however, was girt on all sides by a close belt of trees. In the middle appeared a black marble monument, surmounted by a gracefully sculptured personification of Africa weeping under her palm tree. Near it was seated an old man in black robes, and beside him stood a harp whose chords were still vibrating with recent melody.

'Manfred,' said Crashie, advancing and warmly embracing him, 'what has called you to this dwelling place of sad recollections?'

'A new affliction, my brother, which will overwhelm the soul of one here present with a darker tide of sorrow than did that long past grief which this tomb commemorates.'

'What do you mean, venerable Father?' said the Duke of Wellington, approaching. 'Your mysterious words have sent a strange chill to my heart.'

'I will tell you, but steel your soul for a fearful blow. That son who was your pride and glory, in whom all your hopes and affections were centred, is dead. The Marquis of Douro lies a cold corpse within this lofty mausoleum.'

'Father,' said the Duke hurriedly, 'you dream, you dream! I left my son scarcely a week since in perfect health.'

'Brother, you know,' said the magician, turning to Crashie. 'Have I spoken truly?'

'Too truly,' was the reply, while a tear trickled down the speaker's aged cheek. Such a corroboration left no further room for doubt. An ashy paleness immediately overspread his countenance, his lips quivered and his eye flashed as he exclaimed, 'The stroke emanates from hell. Heaven would crush no man thus!'

I will not attempt to describe his subsequent anguish. It was far too deep and intense for my feeble pen to venture upon. He continued for a long time in a state of almost absolute despair. Sydney, in the meantime, was scarcely less afflicted, for in the Marquis he had lost his first and only friend. Absorbed in lamenting his untimely death, hardly a single thought of the business which had brought him to Philosopher's Island ever entered his head. Even the feelings of the absent lover were swallowed up in those of the bereaved friend.

One day, after nearly six weeks spent in this melancholy manner, the Duke and Sydney were sitting in one of the apartments of the castle, engaged in sad and silent meditation, when Manfred sent a messenger desiring them instantly to appear before him. On entering the room where he sat, an unexpected scene presented itself. Crashie and the magician were seated in state on two thrones. On one side stood the Marquis of Douro restored to life and bright in pristine beauty and vigour, and on the other Lord Ellrington and Mr Montmorency, the one as handsome and the other as ugly as they had ever been.

The father and son were in an instant locked in each other's arms. Their emotions were at first too powerful for utterance, but the Duke quickly mastered his feelings and, turning to the ancient sages, seemed by his looks to demand an explanation from them. This was soon given in a few words. They informed him that that morning, as they were walking in the Grove of Tears, a terrific peal of thunder had burst directly over their heads. On looking up they perceived the four Chief Genii,[36] who rule the destinies of our world, appearing through an opening in the sky. 'Mortals,' they cried, in a voice louder than the previous thunder, 'we, in our abundant mercy, have been moved to compassion by your oft-repeated and grievous lamentations. The cold corpse in that grave shall breathe again the breath of life, provided you pledge a solemn oath that neither he nor his relatives shall ever take revenge on those who slew him, for it is the mighty Brani's will to revivify both the murders also.' 'We swear,' said they without hesitation, 'that none shall injure one hair of their perjured heads.' No sooner were those words uttered than the Genii vanished amidst the roar of ten thousand thunders. A thick darkness now gathered, and the ground shook and heaved as if an earthquake were rolling beneath. When daylight returned the Marquis appeared standing beside the mausoleum and Lord Ellrington and Mr Montmorency were seen in the act of issuing from the wood.

On the night after this happy denouement, Sydney retired to rest early with his dear Arthur. They lay awake for some time conversing on various interesting topics, but at last the Marquis dropped asleep. Edward tried to follow his example but in vain. His mind was in such a state of pleasing yet unaccountable excitement that he found it impossible to compose himself to slumber. He rose, and, walking to the window, began to gaze on the still silent night. The moon and stars were shining in a sky whose deep clear blue was finely contrasted with a few pearly clouds lying motionless on the lustre-filled air. This scene was beginning to calm his fluttering heart when the chamber door softly opened.

'Edward,' said the Duke, for it was he who entered, 'the hour is come. Follow me.' Sydney obeyed without reply.

They left the castle and proceeded to the Grove of Tears. Not a leaf stirred, not a zephyr whispered as they threaded the solitary woods in perfect silence. They emerged from its over-hanging boughs into the more open glade. The tall gloomy mausoleum rose like a colossal giant in the midst, half-black with dense shadow, and half-brightened by a shower of moonbeams. A sort of door had been formed in the basement or pedestal. This stood open. They entered, and after descending a long spiral staircase, arrived at a wide vault all paved with black marble. In the middle stood a table of the same materials, supported by four carved pillars. On it lay a large coffin covered with a pall of purple velvet embroidered in gold, with a coronet and coat-of-arms. At the head and foot of the coffin were two golden lamps burning with a remarkably pure and clear flame. The Duke now took Edward's hand and, leading him to the table, turned a portion of the pall so as to expose the coffin plate.

'There lies your father,' said he, 'read and learn of what tree you are a scion.'

Trembling with excitement and eagerness, he bent forward. A dense mist overspread his eyes as he read the following inscription: 'Here lies Frederick the Great, Duke of York and King of the Twelves.[37] He was slain at the battle of Rosendale Hill on 24th May, 1810. His deeds need no epitaph.'

'Good God!' he exclaimed, and swooned in the Duke's arms.

With some difficulty he was recovered. On opening his eyes his first words were, 'Have I been dreaming or was it a glorious reality?'

'It was a genuine reality. You are no longer Mr Sydney, but Prince Edward of York.'

'For heaven's sake, I implore Your Grace to explain this wondrous, this almost impossible mystery.'

'Calm yourself, Edward, and I will. Your illustrious father, as you well know, landed on the shores of Africa with a small but brave band of twelve men. He was furiously opposed by the semi-barbarous natives of that country, but he defeated them in almost every action, notwithstanding their immeasurable superiority in numbers. Continuing his triumphant progress, he penetrated as far as the mighty Genii-haunted hills of Jibbel Kumri.[38] Here he encamped for a season, and in these mountains it was that the incidents of his life which chiefly concern you occurred. He had always been pleased to distinguish me with peculiar favour, not from any merit of mine, but from the native goodness of his own generous heart. He called me his friend in peace and his right hand in war. One day, while we lay among the Jibbel Kumri, he invited me to accompany him on a short journey of discovery. Alone and unattended we set out. For many hours we wandered among wild and terrible solitudes, where perhaps the tread of man had never before sounded. As the sun began to decline we descended into a kind of vast hollow. I will not deny that I experienced a sensation similar to fear as I stood at the bottom, and looked up at the tremendous walls closing us in on every side, for the narrow gorge by which we had entered looked only like a scarcely perceptible line of light. Rock rose above rock towering higher and yet higher to the height of nearly a thousand feet. The blue sky seemed to repose on their soaring summits. It appeared to have come down to meet their aspiring embrace half way. While we stood motionless, gazing on the sublime horror of the scene, a sudden wailing cry issued from the rock against which we were both leant, just above our heads, and directly after, a very soft and sweet voice implored assistance in the Spanish tongue. Fortunately we understood that language.

' "Who and what are you?" said Frederick. "I am a captive woman," replied the voice, "and if you are mortals, pray you, in the name of heaven, to rescue me from the power of an evil genius who has stolen me from my country and imprisoned me in this dark, lonely cave."

'We retreated a few steps from the rock, and looked up to see if we could discover any hole or cavern. Not the slightest inequality of surface, however, was visible in the smooth bare precipice towering majestically before us.

'"Lady," said I, "by what sign shall we know the rock in which you are enclosed?"

'"Do you not see me?" said she, "I am looking at you through a wide chink in the cave's mouth against which a stone is rolled!"

'"There is magic in this," said Frederick.

'He had scarcely spoken, before the appearance of the rock totally changed. It became all rough and rugged, and in one part the jaws of a vast cavern yawned horribly wide. A great stone blocked it up, but while we were looking at it and considering how we should remove this formidable impediment, it suddenly moved of its own accord, as if it had been impelled forward by some invisible hand, and rolled crashing and thundering down into the hollow beneath. Frederick then gave me his musket.

'"Stay here, Arthur," said he, "while I go and ascertain what treasure is concealed in yonder gloomy casket."

'The rock was not difficult of ascent, so I did not offer to accompany him. In a little while I beheld him returning with a lady whose beauty exceeded everything I have seen before or since. She had that rich dark cast of loveliness, that air of graceful majesty which chiefly belongs to natives of a sunnier clime than that of Britain. When they came up to me she was enthusiastically expressing her gratitude to her gallant deliverer and he, I could perceive, was fully sensible of the value of that gratitude.

'"Beautiful lady," said he, "will you go with me to my camp, or is there any other part of Africa to which I can assist you to fly?"

'"I will go with you," said she, "and let us hasten our departure, for the day is drawing to the close, and at sunset the genius always makes his appearance. If he should find you here – Oh! I tremble to think of the consequences that would ensue."

'It was near midnight before we arrived at the camp. Your father ordered a tent to be instantly prepared for the lady and appointed six African women, whom we had taken captive in a late skirmish, to wait upon her. In a few hours all was profound silence. The men, who had been disturbed at our arrival, were again retired to rest, and everyone was now sunk in the still oblivion of sleep. At this crisis a terrific cry, which might be supposed to resemble the shrill summons of the last trumpet, shook heaven and earth. All started instantly from their beds and rushed into the open air. Hovering over the camp we saw a huge, indistinct form, surrounded with a halo of a dull, fiery red hue, and breathing flames from what seemed to be its mouth.

'"It is the genius!" exclaimed the lady, who had likewise been startled from her sleep, and, overcome with terror, she fainted away. Frederick caught her as she fell and, delivering her to the charge of her attendants, directed them to carry her back to the tent.

'"Presumptuous mortal," exclaimed the genius, "take the punishment due to theft."

'As he spoke or rather yelled these words, a mighty sword glittered in the clear moonbeams. Thrice he brandished it round his head and, at every circle, a noise like the rushing of a whirlwind was heard. Then, lifting his hand, he prepared to blot your father from the number of living men. At that fearful juncture, a voice loud and clear, but silver sweet, was heard saying "Danhasch, Danhasch,[39] by the throne of Solomon I command thee to forbear." This adjuration was repeated three times, and at the last the evil genius vanished from our sight. In his stead appeared a female form of superhuman beauty and stature. She descended perpendicularly to the earth and alighting before your father, she said, "I am Maimoune, the great fairy. At your first landing on the shores of this wide continent I was commanded by the four Genii sovereigns to take you under the shadow of my protection. It is by my aid that you have gone on ever victorious, that you have been delivered from the innumerable dangers which beset your path. I watched over you this day in the haunted Dell of Danger where no mortal foot ever before trod, or ever will again. I disenchanted the cavern where the captive lay, and rolled away the stone. I assisted you to ascend and descend the rock in which it was hollowed, and now I give you her whom you have delivered for a wife."

'Frederick fell on his face, but before he could articulate a word of thanks, the fairy had passed away. Your father and Zorayda (for that was the Spanish lady's name) were united a month afterwards. During two years their life was one continued scene of bliss. No martial alarms came to disturb Zorayda with fears for her husband's safety, as the pacific Kashna[40] then swayed the sceptre of Ashantee and, instead of harassing us by predatory incursions on our rising settlement, that mild and good sovereign entered into a strict alliance with us. In this happy period you were born, but, soon after you saw the light, Kashna died, and the warlike Sai Too Too ascended his father's throne. No further attention was then paid to treaties however sacred, to oaths however solemn. Frederick remonstrated, but in vain. One act of aggression followed another and at last he was compelled to assume arms in self-defence.

'After many engagements, in some of which we were victorious, and in others defeated, the enemy retired to the mountainous and almost inaccessible country round Coomassie. Here we followed them. For some time they refused to venture on a drawn battle, but, by a series of skilful manoeuvres, our leader compelled them to choose between the two alternatives of fighting or starvation. They chose the former, and the hostile armies accordingly drew up on the plain near Rosendale Hill. I need not describe the battle which then took place. Every child has read or heard of it. Your father displayed a degree of daring, magnanimous courage which exalted him in my eyes to something more than human. His white plume was seen ever waving where the battle raged bloodiest and thickest. With my own eyes I saw upwards of a hundred strokes aimed at him from as many quarters, but all were turned away as if by an invisible hand. At last, as he was charging for the twenty-first time at the head of our last body of cavalry, his star-like crest sank suddenly among a dark, circling cloud of foes. I saw the ominous eclipse filled with horror. I rushed forwards. My arm was then nerved with a giant's strength. All who ventured to oppose me were cut to pieces without mercy. In five minutes I was kneeling beside your dying father. The breath of life was fast ebbing through his chilled and livid lips, but his garments were unstained by the slightest trace of blood.

'"Dear Frederick," said I, grasping his death-cold hand, "where are you wounded?"

'"No mortal weapon has touched me," he replied, "but my heart is withered. The springs of life are frozen within me at the touch of some vindictive spirit."

'He paused, yet his lips moved as if he were still endeavouring to speak. I bent lower. Some indistinct murmurs reached my ear but the words, "Arthur – my wife – my child!" were alone audible. I looked again, and he was dead.'

Here the Duke stopped. The emotions which this sad narrative had excited were too powerful to allow of his proceeding. He indulged his grief in silence for a few moments, and then resumed the relation thus:

'The next morning's sun rose over a bloody field. Ten thousand slaughtered Africans lay cold and stiff beneath it. But instead of triumphant songs, the wail of lamentation was heard all through our victorious host. Every man, even the meanest, had lost in Frederick a king, a father, a brother, a bosom friend, and how in such bereavement could they think of glory? When your gentle mother heard the news, she never smiled more. For a few weeks she strove for her child's sake to bear up against the overwhelming affliction, but her efforts were vain. In less than two months she joined her husband in a better world. I took you, now a desolate orphan, under my protection. It afforded me a sort of mournful pleasure to trace in your slight infantile features the noble lineaments of your dead father. But even this consolation was not long permitted me. One day I left you in my tent, under the care of an African boy, sleeping in a sort of cradle or basket, and covered with Frederick's crimson mantle. I had not been long absent when a voice whispered to me, "Return. Return." I instantly obeyed the mysterious mandate. Quashie met me at the tent door. He was weeping and wringing his hands as if in despair.

'"What is the matter?" said I. "Has anything befallen Edward?"

'"He is gone," replied the boy.

'"Gone! Where and how?"

'He then informed me that while he was sitting and watching you as you slept, a vast and cloudy hand had suddenly appeared through an opening in the ground and, seizing the cradle, had vanished as it came. Thus the last sapling of a once mighty tree was blighted and destroyed. Years rolled on. The gallant band of twelve adventurers grew into a great nation. A proud city rose on the desert shores of Guinea. A thousand ships sailed the sea which their little bark crossed alone. Frederick's name was become the burden of legendary song and the theme of twilight tradition, and your transient existence was numbered amongst forgotten things, when one night, about three months since, as I was sitting in the library reading, the apparition of a lovely female figure suddenly rose before me. I directly recognised the fairy Maimoune in the unearthly beauty of her countenance.

'"Mortal," said she, folding her transparent wings and gliding towards me, "the dark river of Destiny rolls on unchecked. Frederick fell by the accursed city. I could not save him. Fate favoured Danhasch and by his hand he died. His child still remained, and over him I stretched my protecting arms. The wicked genius snatched him from me; he would have killed him likewise, had not Destiny interposed her high degree. He was left forsaken in the distant Isle of Britain. There I watched over, cherished and guarded him. And, after the lapse of many years, I have brought him back to his fatherland. Go this night to the beach beneath your palace and you shall see the son of your friend."

'Maimoune then went on to appraise me that Mr Sydney, the young orator, was in reality no other than Prince Edward of York. Having communicated this information she proceeded thus: "Danhasch will yet have power to harm him unless you and the two wondrous brothers Crashie and

Manfred accompany him to his father's tomb on the night which precedes the anniversary of Rosendale Hill. There open the coffin, cut from the head of the corpse a lock of hair and with magic ceremonies, form it into an amulet. So long as he wears this charm next to his heart the blight of misfortune can never approach him."

'When Maimoune had vanished, I immediately repaired to the sea beach. Here I found you wandering about disconsolately enough. The strong resemblance which you bore to Frederick struck me forcibly, for, though your form and features are much less manly than his, yet they are cast in the same noble and intellectual mould. I need not say any more. The events which followed are well known to you.'

As the Duke ceased to speak, Manfred and Crashie entered the vault, one bearing a vessel of fire and the other a large book clasped with gold. They placed the vessel at the head of the coffin and Manfred, taking his station beside it, opened the book and began to read from it in an unknown tongue. In a little while the coffin moved. The pall fell aside and the lid slowly uplifted. The corpse was now visible, wrapped in its shroud, clay-cold and rigid, but all untouched by the wasting finger of decay. Crashie approached. There was one glossy ringlet lying on the still marble brow. He severed it with scissors and, uttering a single word, the lid and pall returned to their places again, concealing the pale image of death. He then threw the lock into the vessel of fire; a bright transparent flame instantly rose from it as high as the roof. This burnt with transparent brilliancy for some time, but, quickly exhausting itself, it sank again. Some sparkling substance was now seen among the embers. It was a little locket or brooch in which a small portion of hair appeared under a very rich diamond. Crashie took it from the ashes and, approaching Edward, said,

'Wear this, my son, ever at you heart. It will preserve you from many evils.'

The necessary ceremonies being thus completed, the Prince and Duke left the vault. It was already morning; the first beams were gilding the dark summit of the mausoleum. When Edward returned to his apartment in the castle, he found the Marquis risen.

'Have you been sleepwalking tonight, Ned?' he exclaimed gaily. He received in answer a relation of all that had occurred during the last four hours. His account excited more pleasure than surprise in the Marquis's mind.

'I do not feel much astonished at what you have just told me,' said he, 'for I always felt convinced that your birth and rank were of the very highest order.'

In two days all the party, including Lord Ellrington and Mr Montmorency, left the Philosopher's Island. During the voyage homewards the Duke became acquainted with all the circumstances of the Prince's attachment to his niece. He assured him that nothing was now to be apprehended from her father's opposition to their union.

After a prosperous voyage of six days they reached Verdopolis on the very night of Julia's intended sacrifice. It was their vessel which she had seen approaching the shore while sitting at her lattice. On arriving at Waterloo Palace they learnt from the servants what was going on in the private chapel. Thither the Duke, Marquis and Prince immediately repaired. (Crashie had left them before and was returned to the Tower of All Nations). Their opportune interference prevented all unpleasant consequences which might have arisen from Julia's firmly expressed resolution never to accept Sir James as a husband. And when an explanation of all the above circumstances had duly taken place, the Marquis

114

of Wellesley ceased to throw obstacles in the way of his daughter's happiness.

As soon as the return of the absentees, including our great patriarch, became generally known, the disaffection which had caused so much tumult in the city was instantly quelled.

Three weeks after, the Lady Julia became the Princess Julia. Her royal husband, who now in right of his birth received an annual income of two hundred thousand pounds from government, purchased a splendid villa in the lovely valley of Verdopolis. There the happy couple retired to spend the honeymoon, and there we shall now leave them in the enjoyment of all the happiness which wealth, beauty and virtue can bestow.

I must not, however, close this tedious narrative without giving my reader some information respecting the future lot of the rejected suitor. His Grace of Wellington, pitying poor Sir Jemmy's destitute condition, employed all his influence to move the tender heart of Lady Selina Cathcart, a well-known fashionable belle, to take compassion on him. This she was easily induced to do, for the Baronet's fair estate and deep purse were matrimonial considerations not to be lightly passed over. They were accordingly married and lived ever after as happily as could be expected.

NOTES

1. Captain Tree was one of Charlotte's early pseudonyms.

2. Verdopolis is Greek for 'glass town', the name the Brontës adopted for the setting of much of their juvenilia.

3. Here, Brontë is referring to Lord Charles Wellesley – another of her early pseudonyms, and the narrator of *The Green Dwarf*. Charlotte created a bitter literary rivalry between the personae of Captain Tree and Wellesley throughout her juvenilia.

4. One of several words which Charlotte used for 'fairy'.

5. A northern England form of the Scottish word 'bairn' meaning 'child'.

6. An old Etonian tradition in which 'salt', i.e. money, was collected in support of the captain of the school at Cambridge.

7. In the Brontës' juvenilia, Verdopolis, formerly called Great Glass Town, is set in the Bay of Glass Town, at the mouth of the Niger in the Gulf of the Guinea.

8. This is the Brontës' equivalent to the biblical Tower of Babel.

9. Bravey was one of the original Twelves – a set of twelve toy soldiers, belonging to Branwell Brontë as a child. The Twelves inspired many of the Brontës' stories.

10. This poem is written in the 'old young men tongue', a language imitating Yorkshire dialect which was invented by Branwell for his twelve toy soldiers, also known as his twelve 'Young Men'.

11. In the Brontës' stories, Pigtail was a notorious Frenchman known for stealing, torturing and killing children.

12. Arthur Wellesley, the Marquis of Douro, is a prominent member of society in Verdopolis.

13. Lord Ellrington is Alexander Percy, also known as Alexander Rogue, an implacable enemy of the Marquis of Douro.

14. Captain Arbor is the foremost literary figure in Verdopolis.

15. 'Senior wrangler' is a term from the University of Cambridge for the person who achieves highest place in the mathematical tripos.

16. See note 13.

17. Valiant or courageous through drink.

18. A heeltap is a peg in the heel of the shoe which is removed when the shoe is finished. A person leaving any drink in his glass is often told to 'take off his heeltap'.

19. The charioteer of Achilles.

20. Frederic Lofty is a good friend of the Marquis of Douro and an accomplished horseman. He appears elsewhere in the juvenilia.

21. Lady Zenobia Ellrington is the wife of Alexander Rogue, Lord Ellrington.

22. The Rotunda is the place where the noblemen of Verdopolis gather to exchange views.

23. Methuselah was the oldest man in the Bible (Genesis 5: 27).

24. Deriving from weighing scales, the term 'kick the beam' refers to when one object greatly outweighs another.

25. Montmorency is a Verdopolitan nobleman and the evil mentor of Lord Ellrington.

26. Meaning 'to advance at a steady pace'.

27. This poem echoes Byron's 'Lachin Y Gair' (1807) both in content and in metre.

28. Lady Ellrington's brothers, all fops.

29. Vitriol or ferrous sulphate, used in dyeing, tanning and making ink.

30. These are the ruling sovereigns of Verdopolis.

31. Crashie is the patriarch and spiritual power of Verdopolis, who resides in the Tower of All Nations.

32. Gravey is one of the original Twelves (see note 9), and a hero in Emily Brontë's juvenilia.

33. Rebels who occur elsewhere in the juvenilia.

34. Captain John Ross is originally a character in Anne Brontë's juvenilia.

35. This is the magician Manfred, president of the Philosopher's Island, and brother of Crashie.

36. The four chief Genii, Tali, Brani, Emi and Anni, were Charlotte, Branwell, Emily and Anne Brontë respectively.

37. Charlotte most probably based this character on the contemporary Duke of York; Prince Frederick, Duke of York and Albany (1763–1827), was the second son of King George III. As commander-in-chief of the British Army, he presided over the unsuccessful 1793–8 Flanders campaign during the French Revolutionary Wars. He is now mainly remembered as the inspiration behind the nursery rhyme 'The Grand Old Duke of York'.

38. The Jibbel Kumri hills lie at the source of the Nile, to the east of Fernando Po in the Gulf of Guinea. This was the site the Brontës chose as the centre of their African kingdom.

39. In the story of 'Camaralzaman and Badoura', from *Arabian Nights*, Princess Badoura was placed on Prince Camaralzaman's bed to compare their claims to beauty. The fairy Maimoune changed herself into a flea and bit the prince on the neck in order to awake him. Danhasch, an evil genie, changed himself into a flea and bit the princess on the lip, so that she too might wake and see the prince.

40. In the Brontës' imaginary world, Kashna Quamina was the King of Ashantee. He was succeeded by his son Sai Too Too, who continued the first Ashantee Wars until his death at the Battle of Coomassie. (Coomassie was the capital of Ashantee.)

BIOGRAPHICAL NOTE

Charlotte Brontë was born in Thornton, Yorkshire, in 1816. In 1820 her father was appointed curate at Haworth and the family moved to Haworth Parsonage, where Charlotte was to spend most of her life. Following the death of her mother in 1821 and of her two eldest sisters in 1825, she and her two surviving sisters, Emily and Anne, and brother, Branwell, were brought up by their father and a devoutly religious aunt.

Theirs was an unhappy childhood, in particular the period the sisters spent at a school for daughters of the clergy. Charlotte abhorred the harsh regime, blaming it for the death of her two sisters, and she went on to fictionalise her experiences there in *Jane Eyre*. Having been removed from the school, the three sisters, together with Branwell, found solace in storytelling. Inspired by a set of toy soldiers, they created the imaginary kingdoms of Angria and Gondal, which form the settings for much of their juvenilia. From 1831 to 1832 Charlotte was educated at Roe Head school, where she later returned as a teacher.

In 1842 Charlotte travelled to Brussels with Emily. They returned home briefly following the death of their aunt, but, soon after, Charlotte was back in Brussels, this time as a teacher. At great expense, the three sisters published a volume of poetry – *Poems by Currer, Ellis and Acton Bell* (1846) – but this proved unsuccessful, selling only two copies. By the time of its publication, each of the sisters had completed a novel: Emily's *Wuthering Heights*, and Anne's *Agnes Grey* were both published in 1847, but Charlotte's novel, *The Professor*, remained unpublished in her lifetime. Undeterred, Charlotte embarked on *Jane Eyre*, which was also published in 1847 and hailed by Thackeray as 'the masterwork of a great genius'. She followed this up with *Shirley* (1849) and *Villette* (1853), and continued to be published under the pseudonym Currer Bell although her identity was, by now, well known.

Branwell, in many ways the least successful of the four siblings, died in 1848. His death deeply distressed the sisters, and both Emily and Anne died within the following year. Charlotte married her father's curate in 1854, but she died in the early stages of pregnancy in March 1855.

SELECTED TITLES FROM HESPERUS PRESS

Author	Title	Foreword writer
Louisa May Alcott	*Behind a Mask*	Doris Lessing
Jane Austen	*Love and Friendship*	Fay Weldon
Honoré de Balzac	*Colonel Chabert*	A.N. Wilson
Aphra Behn	*The Lover's Watch*	
Giovanni Boccaccio	*Life of Dante*	A.N. Wilson
Charlotte Brontë	*The Green Dwarf*	Libby Purves
Emily Brontë	*Poems of Solitude*	Helen Dunmore
Mikhail Bulgakov	*The Fatal Eggs*	Doris Lessing
Geoffrey Chaucer	*The Parliament of Birds*	
Wilkie Collins	*The Frozen Deep*	
Wilkie Collins	*Who Killed Zebedee?*	Martin Jarvis
Arthur Conan Doyle	*The Mystery of Cloomber*	
William Congreve	*Incognita*	Peter Ackroyd
Joseph Conrad	*Heart of Darkness*	A.N. Wilson
Joseph Conrad	*The Return*	Colm Tóibín
Dante Alighieri	*New Life*	Louis de Bernières
Daniel Defoe	*The King of Pirates*	Peter Ackroyd
Charles Dickens	*The Haunted House*	Peter Ackroyd
Charles Dickens	*A House to Let*	
Fyodor Dostoevsky	*The Double*	Jeremy Dyson
George Eliot	*Amos Barton*	Matthew Sweet
Henry Fielding	*Jonathan Wild the Great*	Peter Ackroyd
F. Scott Fitzgerald	*The Rich Boy*	John Updike
E.M. Forster	*Arctic Summer*	Anita Desai
Giuseppe Garibaldi	*My Life*	Tim Parks
Elizabeth Gaskell	*Lois the Witch*	Jenny Uglow
Johann Wolfgang von Goethe	*The Man of Fifty*	A.S. Byatt
Thomas Hardy	*Fellow-Townsmen*	Emma Tennant

L.P. Hartley	*Simonetta Perkins*	Margaret Drabble
Nathaniel Hawthorne	*Rappaccini's Daughter*	Simon Schama
Henry James	*In the Cage*	Libby Purves
Franz Kafka	*Metamorphosis*	Martin Jarvis
John Keats	*Fugitive Poems*	Andrew Motion
D.H. Lawrence	*Daughters of the Vicar*	Anita Desai
D.H. Lawrence	*The Fox*	Doris Lessing
Jack London	*Before Adam*	
Katherine Mansfield	*In a German Pension*	Linda Grant
Edgar Lee Masters	*Spoon River Anthology*	
Guy de Maupassant	*Butterball*	Germaine Greer
Sir Thomas More	*The History of King Richard III*	Sister Wendy Beckett
Sándor Petőfi	*John the Valiant*	George Szirtes
Alexander Pope	*The Rape of the Lock and A Key to the Lock*	Peter Ackroyd
Alexander Pope	*Scriblerus*	Peter Ackroyd
Marcel Proust	*Pleasures and Days*	A.N. Wilson
Alexander Pushkin	*Dubrovsky*	Patrick Neate
Mary Shelley	*Transformation*	
Percy Bysshe Shelley	*Zastrozzi*	Germaine Greer
Robert Louis Stevenson	*Dr Jekyll and Mr Hyde*	Helen Dunmore
Jonathan Swift	*Directions to Servants*	Colm Tóibín
W.M. Thackeray	*Rebecca and Rowena*	Matthew Sweet
Leo Tolstoy	*Hadji Murat*	Colm Tóibín
Mark Twain	*The Diary of Adam and Eve*	John Updike
Mark Twain	*Tom Sawyer, Detective*	
Edith Wharton	*The Touchstone*	Salley Vickers
Oscar Wilde	*The Portrait of Mr W.H.*	Peter Ackroyd
Virginia Woolf	*Carlyle's House and Other Sketches*	Doris Lessing
Virginia Woolf	*Monday or Tuesday*	Scarlett Thomas
Emile Zola	*For a Night of Love*	A.N. Wilson